FOREVER FOUND

TERROR, MN SERIES
BOOK 2

LARISSA EMERALD

Forever Found
Terror, MN Series – Novel

Copyright © 2020 Castle Oak Publishing LLC

ISBN-13: 978-1-942139-20-1

http://www.larissaemerald.com

Published in the United States of America.

Books by Larissa Emerald

Paranormal Romance

Divine Tree Guardian Series
Awakening Fire
Awakening Touch
Awakening Storm

Vampire
Forever at Dawn
Forever at Midnight

Terror, MN Paranormal
Forever at Risk
Forever Found

Paranormal Thriller
Perfection

Nocturne Falls Universe
The Vampire Bounty Hunter's Unexpected Catch
The Shaman Charms the Shifter
Merry & Bright Anthology – The Witch's Snow Globe
Wish
The Dragon Falls for the Fairy Godmother

Romantic Suspense
Winter Heat

Contemporary Romance
Come Sail Away – Barefoot Bay Novella

THE STORY

Founded by angels, harassed by demons, the town of Terror, MN is hidden in the northern Minnesota countryside. Obey the rules and it's a fun town. #1 rule: Do NOT eat thy neighbor.

In the world of paranormal creatures, few things are ever final.

Lyndsey Goeig has a psychic connection with her camera. The pictures she takes reveal the truth, and more than the human eye can see. When she's drawn to Terror, MN, to visit her cousin, she finds more than a simple get-away…she encounters the man who rescued her from death when she was a child. Only now he's an angel charged with protecting Terror from outsiders and demons.

Humans have a way of disturbing the balance in the secretive and secluded paranormal town of Terror. Angel David has enough problems keeping the balance among the supernatural residents. To his mind, humans should visit someplace else, including the all-grown-up, intriguing female from his past. He isn't happy when a beautiful Lyndsey snaps pictures, capturing him battling a demon. His concerns escalate when he discovers Lyndsey is part of the reason he died. Plus, the beast that tried to kill her before is determined to succeed time.

Will David rescue her again and find the love between them that is meant to be? Fate may have brought them together, but if they want a chance at a future, they're going to have to fight for it.

Terror, Minnesota

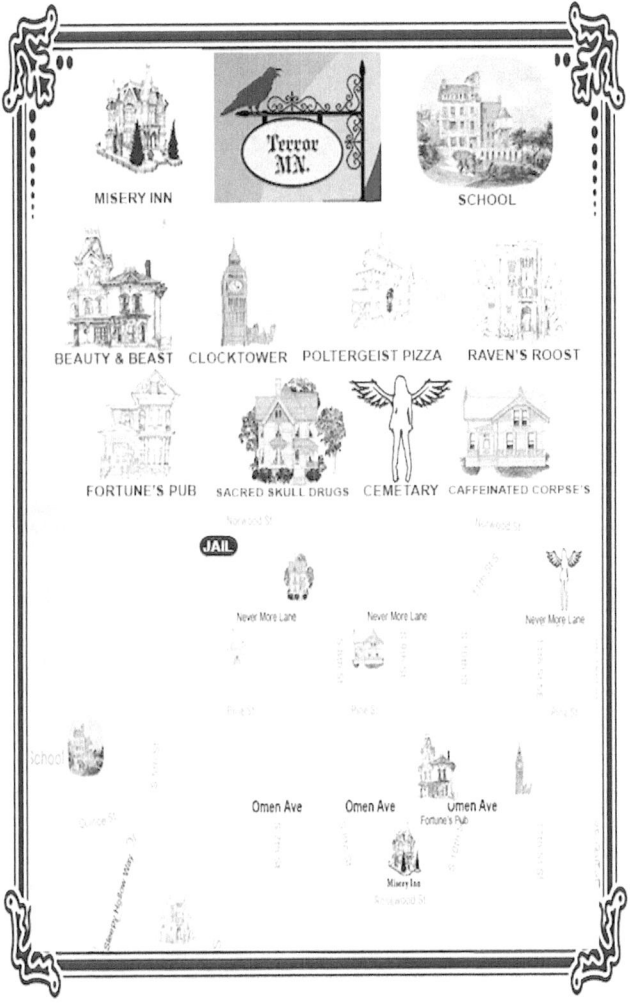

FOREVER FOUND

1

Boxes littered her living room. Like her life, they didn't seem to have any order. She began labeling them with a permanent marker as she peeked inside to remember what she'd packed. Kitchen, bedroom, bath. She stacked them near the doorway.

Her cell phone sounded the crystals ringtone, which meant it was her bestie, Jen. But where was the phone? Lyndsey dug around, following the sound as it led her to the bookshelf, where she spied the glow of the screen next to the pile of photo albums. She plucked the phone up, then answered, "Hey, girl. What's up?"

"Just keeping track of you. How's it going?" Jen asked.

Lyndsey Goeig drew in a silent, deep breath. "Good. Good. I'm almost finished packing. Then John, a friend from work, well, you know, work before I got laid off, will help me haul this stuff to storage."

"I'm glad you have someone to help. Have you decided where you're going yet? The offer still stands to hang with me for a while until you figure out what's next."

"I know. I appreciate the offer." But Jen, as much as Lyndsey adored her friend, had her quirks. Just because they were best friends didn't mean they'd make good roommates. Jen was a type-A personality with a side of anxiety disorder, and Lyndsey was a type-B with a touch of ADD. They would drive each other crazy. Besides, Jen lived in a busy part of town. *Not for me.*

Lyndsey thumbed through some loose pictures, then added them to the group at her feet. Her heart squeezed as she dropped cross-legged to the floor, tugging another empty box closer. She placed the picture albums of her childhood in the container that would go into storage until she figured out where she was going. She was young, free, and had her entire life in front of her. Her choices were endless. These were the things she told herself in those moments of panic.

In reality, she'd been laid off from her photography job at the newspaper, her apartment had been bought out by a big-wig industrial company, and today was move-out day. In one way, the timing couldn't have been better. She could go wherever the wind took her—the lousy thing was…no wind.

"Let me know if you want to brainstorm jobs, or if I can help," Jen said.

"I will. I'm just going to concentrate on freelance work for a while. Thanks for checking on me. Bye." Lyndsey ran her finger over the end button, chewing her lower lip. She thrived on change, right? She always had. Lucky Lyndsey.

She lifted another album, then leaned to drop it into the box. The cover fell open, revealing a snapshot of her and her cousin Justin during the Winter Carnival in St. Paul. They stood beside the enormous ice sculptures. She must have been around sixteen. Those were fun times.

As she held the picture, a tingling raced from her hand up her arm and into her chest. It dissolved in an instant. But she understood the feeling had something to do with the picture. The imprint drew her. She wondered why. Justin lived north of St. Paul in Terror, Minnesota. She hadn't seen him in years. They kept up on Facebook, but that was it.

She stared at the photo as a strong pull, like the force of a magnet, tugged at her spirit, her very core. She saw real things in pictures. Sometimes, it was auras. Other times, just something other people didn't see. Once or twice, the camera had done weird stuff like burning a hole in a bedspread. Those instances had blown her away. Unexplainably, she felt compelled to visit Justin. Life had taught her to listen to these mystical sensations.

Placing the rest of the photo albums in the box, she sealed it, labeled it *photos*, and set it with the rest of her belongings.

Call Justin. Find out what is driving this connection sensation.

She hesitated. Finally, she found Justin in her contacts and dialed.

When he answered, she felt a little awkward. "Hi, Justin. This is your cousin, Lyndsey."

"Lucky Lyndsey. How have you been?"

She remembered now he was the one who had called her that. "Great. How about you?"

After they exchanged pleasantries, she paused, building her courage. "I'm doing some traveling up your way, and I wondered if I could drop by for a little while. Do you have room for a guest?"

"Sure. Of course. Come on."

"Awesome. I'll be there on Tuesday. Thanks. I can't wait to catch up." Or to discover what was driving her to him after all these years. She ended the call, glancing at her photography paraphernalia. Her equipment was all she needed to survive.

Have camera, will travel.

You're not the hero you think you are.

David stared at the note scrawled in demon blood he'd unfurled from the mailbox. The letters were written over one another in different strokes and multiple shades from red to black. Perhaps to camouflage the script? Maybe to make it almost illegible. Almost. Probably because the demon who wrote it was fixated on a point. He flipped the paper over.

It's time to settle the score.

He stretched the sudden ache in his wings, then curled them tightly into place as he stared beyond the lawn of Thurston Mansion, the home of the Angel Alliance, the residence of the angels who were charged with keeping peace in Terror. A significant part of their job was to bind demonic powers and principalities.

The message wasn't addressed to anyone in particular, but it was meant for him. David understood that.

Of course, you aren't a hero, the voice in his head immediately assured him. He'd never thought he was. And what score were they talking about?

Glimpses of another time, of another life—before he'd been assigned this angel gig—flashed in his mind. He caught snippets of him running into the street and pushing a woman with a stroller out of the path of an oncoming dump truck. The vehicle had struck him, sending him flying through the air. He didn't recall landing.

He'd been thirty-four when he'd died. He'd been at the right spot at the right time to save them as he walked along the street to meet a friend for lunch. After being assigned his angel duties, he'd learned the woman and her three-year-old little girl were safe. They'd only suffered a few bumps and bruises. But for him, it had been his admission to becoming an angel—the selfless act of giving his life to save someone else's. It hadn't been intentional, though. He'd simply reacted…and boom, that was it. He was reasonably sure that was what the note referred to. No, he wasn't a hero.

Regardless, a demon had a beef about *something*, and the beast had figured out where he lived. But which demon? Not one of the new residents of Terror—the town attracted all kinds of supernaturals. But demons weren't welcome.

David considered the note. Was that a *C* scribbled at the bottom? He angled the page, trying to get better light. A name came to him as he did so. *Caleb?* The demon who had run him down, who was the reason David had died and was an angel today?

The missive ignited, the letters sizzling, burning, then disintegrating into ash that fell from his fingers, dotting the snow with black soot.

He wondered what this was about after all these years. Why now?

Behind him, the snow crunched beneath tires. He turned his head as Rylan Lewis drove his Hummer next to him and stopped, rolling down the window. The building contractor had arrived for their meeting to look over the construction of the new gymnasium.

"Our appointment still on?" Rylan asked.

"Yes." David rubbed his fingertips together to release any lingering particles of ash, then clasped the other letters. He waved it slightly. "Just getting some fresh air and the mail."

Rylan nodded. "Hop in, and we'll head up the drive."

David did, knowing Rylan would otherwise be left waiting on him. It was a long drive to the house.

At the top of the circle driveway in front of the mansion, Rylan threw the vehicle into park and turned off the ignition. "Something wrong?" he asked.

David paused, averting his eyes away from the lion shifter. "No."

"Gotcha."

They both exited the Hummer, then walked up the steps to the mansion—one of the perks of his life as an angel. "We'll go through the house to get to the gym."

After depositing the mail on the counter, he continued toward the back of the house. Out the window, he noticed Grady, the butler and house organizer extraordinaire, talking with three of the other angels who lived there. They were probably putting in their requests for the shopping list.

David didn't feel like continuing with the meet-up. He wanted to step away and contemplate the threatening message. But that was life. He often had to suck it up and do things he didn't want to do even when he wasn't alive in the traditional sense.

"You didn't look at it already, did you?" Rylan asked.

"What? No. You asked me to wait. So I did."

Entering the new gymnasium, David expanded his wings, allowing them to test the breadth, taking up about half the width of the basketball court. Excellent. There was a lot of space. He took in the shiny wooden floors, inhaling the fresh scent of polyurethane that hung in the air. "Your crew did an outstanding job. The gym is exactly the way the angels need it—massive, with extra room on the sidelines and a soaring ceiling. The row of windows high up near the ceiling let in great light." His voice echoed, bouncing off the folded bleachers and walls covered with black-and-teal mats.

Rylan shoved his hands into his pockets, nodding. "Thanks. I knew it would come together. It was a bit dicey when I had to make a trip to Nocturne Falls around Halloween, but, since I've been back, everything has run like clockwork. The shell, meaning the framework and roof, was completed before the first snow, so we were able to do finish work from there on out."

"You said you added something special?"

"Yeah. Right. That's in the weight room. It isn't quite finished, but let's take a look," Rylan said, leading the way.

The lion shifter headed to the back corner of the court, then exited through a rear door. He moved across a short hall and into another room, this one almost the size of the basketball court but filled with equipment—the dream obstacle course for a supernatural. Weights and barbells sat at one end. Those were the only items that spoke of a standard weight room. The rest could be a setting for a parkour training facility with half walls, beams, bars, and climbing walls in all manner of configurations to jump, flip, and fly over.

"Oh, wow. This is going to become *the* place. Awesome, man. Thanks." He couldn't wait to run off some tension in here himself.

"The allies will be thrilled." The allied angels need a lot of outlets for their pent-up energy. This should help. At times, it was darn frustrating to stand by and watch what idiot humans and supernaturals chose to do. But there were rules, and they weren't allowed to interfere with or engage in the troubled instances the earth's population found themselves in. The angels were there for duty first—to keep balance within Terror—not on a vacay.

"Since we're deep in winter, this will be great." And maybe the angels could simply hibernate in the mansion all winter…in peace and quiet.

The road was slippery as Lyndsey drove along Sleepy Hollow Way. What a name for a street. Then again, the town *was* called Terror. Her stomach clenched as a bad feeling trickled through her. She tightened her grip on the steering wheel. That was ridiculous.

Still, she couldn't shake the nervous squeeze she'd had in her belly since she had crossed the city-limits sign.

Something awful is going to happen today.

Lyndsey blinked as her tires hit a patch of black ice, slid, and then regained traction. She wondered if she were going to crash—if maybe that was the reason for her anxiety or an additional purpose for why she was in Terror in the first place. Having a sixth sense didn't mean the reasons why were clear. She looked around for a sign. But the blue sky outside her window appeared as they did any other day. She eyed the high school as she drove past. When she reached Nevermore Lane, the traffic light turned red. She stopped, then glanced at her phone to check the GPS. Maps weren't working, and Justin's house was off the grid. She sighed.

To the right, several crows perched on a for-sale sign in front of an old Victorian house. They watched her with their beady eyes.

She shuddered, an unreasonable fear setting in. The light changed, and she rolled on. The birds followed, flying alongside her car. Soon after, she passed the sheriff's office. At least that meant they had law enforcement here. She'd heard wild things about Terror…tales of people disappearing. She shook her head, not quite sure where that thought had come from.

Her tires skidded on the pavement again.

Maybe she should have put on snow chains, but since it was only the first week of December, she'd figured she had more time before she needed them. With snow chains, the beautiful ride upstate would have been bumpy and noisy. As it was, the main highway had been clear of snow. Just those couple of patches of ice so far.

After passing a dense thicket of trees, a massive gothic mansion came into view. She slowed, checking her rearview mirror for traffic before steering across the street into the mansion's driveway. A set of gorgeous wrought-iron gates stood open at the entry. She glanced at her camera, where it rested on the passenger seat. It was where she always kept it when she was en route somewhere. A great shot could materialize when least expected—like this one.

Lyndsey drove right on in, scanning the area for a place to get the best picture of the old building. She parked the car, grabbed her camera, and got out. A chance at an awesome image was always worth the risk of getting yelled at or thrown off the premises. And she trusted her gut as to which pictures were worth the extra effort.

As she got out, she searched for the crows. They had gathered in the trees. She could feel them watching her.

Stepping away from her car, she assessed the space. The mansion had spectacular lines. The outer wings jutted forward, framing the central main entrance. A turret with bay windows accented the left side. On the right, there was a mixture of large rectangular windows. The center section had arched cathedral windows. Low, neatly trimmed hedges were covered with snow.

She snapped a few frames, pausing briefly to adjust the camera settings for different shots. Through the lens, she noticed two men strolling toward her from the manse. Zooming in, she kept clicking pictures as the men advanced. One guy was quite built, with dark hair streaked with platinum. The impression of someone being struck by lightning flashed in her mind. Jerking his head to the side, he swept his hair out of his eyes. The other man was also big, but he had golden hair. His fluid steps suggested he was calmer, perhaps less bothered by her presence.

"Hey," the dark-haired man snapped. "No pictures on my property."

Lyndsey couldn't stop the pressure of her finger as she clicked once more as he halted near her. She drew her camera down beside her thigh. "I'm sorry." But she wasn't. "The building intrigued me. And when I get that feeling—" She paused, placing her palm on her stomach "—I just have to capture it. How old is it?"

"I do not authorize the use of those photos," the owner said, ignoring her question. He moved his head, revealing a long scar marring his cheek. That must have hurt. It didn't detract from his striking good looks, though. If anything, it made his cheekbones and strong jaw more prominent. His long-sleeved shirt clung to his refined muscles. He should've been wearing a coat, but she wasn't about to argue with his choice. The man had an excellent physique.

She shrugged a shoulder. "I mean no harm. The photos are merely for my pleasure, Mister…?"

"I'm David Snyder." He tipped his body slightly in a rather formal move.

When he looked at her, his eyes suddenly filled her universe. She tore her gaze away.

"Rylan Lewis," the other man acknowledged.

"I'm Lyndsey Goeig. I'm heading to visit my cousin for a few weeks. Justin Smith? You may know him." Still talking, she began walking to her car. She'd learned that most of the time, it was better to leave quickly before anyone thought to ask for her memory card. "I saw this place, and I had to grab a few shots." She opened the driver's side door. One glossy black crow flew over, then perched on the top edge of the doorframe.

She jumped backward, a shriek catching in her throat. Regaining her composure, she lifted her camera, zeroing in on the menacing bird. It turned its head toward her, opening and closing its sharp beak as if posing. She took a photo, then glanced back at the man.

"Wait," David said, eyeing all the stuff she had crammed in the backseat. "Do you have any ID?"

"Of course." Then, to the bird, she said, "Shoo! Go away." She fanned her free hand at the car door. The crow flew off.

After she carefully set the camera on the passenger's seat, she tugged the driver's seat forward to get her purse, which was perched on a precarious stack of her belongings. As she did, the mound of items—a thermos, tripod, jacket, and more—spilled into a messy pile on the floor. She stood, huffing in frustration.

David crossed his arms and waited, a disapproving

scowl furrowing his brow. She'd seen that look before when her mother had stepped into her bedroom, fussing over clothes on the floor. And when her last boyfriend had seen her office desk. And then again when her friend Jen had dropped by, and Lyndsey's kitchen table had been taken over by her latest project. The fact was, she tended to be a messy person. Her brain worked best in a state of chaos. She'd made peace with it a long time ago. Besides, she would always put things right eventually…for a brief time anyway.

"Um, it slid under my stuff."

The other man, Rylan, checked his phone. "Sorry, I have to run," he said to David, turning and walking briskly to a Hummer parked in the circle section of the driveway.

"Nice to meet you," she said with a wave he didn't catch. Her gaze shifted back to David and his annoyed glare. "I'll be out of your way in just a second." She tossed the thermos, tripod, and jacket back onto the pile. Pushing the seat into place, she pulled her purse free as she did.

Removing her wallet, she showed the man her driver's license. It wasn't a big deal—she often had to prove she wasn't a stalker or something. She considered it good practice for people to know what was going on around them.

Lifting a brow, he stepped back. "Okay. Don't let me find those pictures on display anywhere. The people of Terror, well, we like our privacy."

She hesitated for a moment as she studied him. A strange sensation came over her, a prickling of some memory, of some image, as her scarf brushed against the hair on the nape of her neck. Whatever the picture was, she couldn't grab on to it. She blew out a whoosh of air as she slid behind the steering wheel. "Don't worry. To publish them without permission would be unethical. I don't operate that way. I'll let you know if I use them. I promise."

He gave one sharp nod.

"Would you direct me to Norwood Street, though, please? My GPS stopped working as soon as I crossed into town."

"Turn left at the end of the drive. It's one more street north."

She smiled. "Great. Thanks."

She started the ignition, put the car in gear, and looked around to decide which way to exit. If she took the large circle drive as Rylan had, it would take her closer to the house, which she guessed David wouldn't appreciate much. So she backed up, made a three-point turn, and drove out the way she had entered. At the main road, she turned left as he'd instructed, leaving the crows and the intimidating yet way-too-handsome man behind.

Look what I've been missing. Back from the dungeons of hell, his timing couldn't have been more perfect.

Shifting from crow to his human form, Caleb rubbed his hands together as he watched the woman drive away. All this angst, turmoil, and life. She had been upset over her camera and…something else. He couldn't quite put his finger on what. However, he was out of practice.

Purgatory was the most boring place. Nothing but lessons upon lessons. Heaven or Hell was where the action was at. He'd spent twenty-five years in Purgatory as punishment for his failure in taking the lives of Lyndsey and her mother. Plus, Lucifer still blamed him for allowing David to become another angel. As if Caleb could have had any clue the man was going to run out in front of a dump truck to save them!

Damn that Mountain of Purgatory with its seven terraces of wrath, envy, pride, sloth, lust, gluttony, and greed… Blah, blah, blah. It was a horrible prison for someone who enjoyed vices as Caleb did. The inferno of Hell itself had been much more to his liking. And now Lucifer had allowed him to earn his way back to fun and pleasure.

Retaining his shape as one of the crows, he followed the girl.

David paused inside the massive foyer of Thurston Mansion as the door clicked shut behind him. Lyndsey Goeig? He hadn't heard the name in years, although it seemed a part of her was always with him. It was as if something of her essence had latched onto him in that long-ago instant. She was frozen in time in her fearful, little-girl gaze when her eyes met his as he'd thrust her stroller across the street into safety. She was the baby he'd rescued. Well, she hadn't been a baby, but a three-year-old toddler. That would put her at—he did the mental math—twenty-eight now. And man, she'd grown into a beautiful woman. Her skin glowed beneath a perfect bone structure, and her lips were expressive and slightly full. A chestnut brown with a hint of gold and red hues, her shoulder-length hair was rich and thick. But her eyes were the most alluring…it was as if she could see right into his most guarded secrets.

What was she doing in Terror? And right when the demon Caleb showed up? That couldn't be good or a coincidence. A chill ran through him, settling in his gut. He needed to keep a close eye on her.

Prissy and Ruby, his Pomeranians, rushed to greet him, yipping and barking. He scooped a pup into each hand, then tucked them close to his chest.

"Where do you think you're going?" he asked the pups. Prissy's pink tongue darted out as she panted in delight.

With leisurely steps, David strolled down the hall before entering the family room at the back of the house. He set the dogs in their matching beds with the fluffy pink pillows, then went into the kitchen where he dropped another Starbucks coffee pod in the Keurig and pushed "start." He had told Diego, a wolf shifter and the owner of a motorcycle and repair shop, that he'd stop by today. May as well take a hot cup of Joe for the road.

Whether she was traveling north or not, she couldn't be sure. She lacked that kind of directional compass, preferring to use left and right labels and landmarks to navigate places.

A mile up the road, she came to the sign for Norwood Street and turned right. It was a natural choice since it was the only way she could turn. As she drove along, she noticed the houses were not well marked. There was a charming sidewalk, and the neighborhood was filled with huge old trees. They didn't have mailboxes on the street, and most homes had detached garages. She passed a home that had the number *348* above the door, so she deduced Justin's home was most likely two blocks down. Next, she passed a house numbered *516 ½*. That made her smile. Man, things were crazy in this town. By her best estimate, she guessed Justin's house was three more down. A truck blocked the driveway, so she parked at the curb.

When she reached the front stoop, she peered at the numbers on the mailbox. They were askew and not visible from the street, but they now confirmed she had the correct house—*562*.

She moved up the steps to stand on the old wooden porch, pulling her coat closer around her ears and approached the faded green door. Lifting the brass knocker, she knocked. The wind whooshed by again, lifting a fresh dusting of snow on the lawn and contributing to the white mound piled against the picket fence—a crow perched on a slat of wood, watching her. With a shiver, she knocked again, this time with several taps in quick succession.

Footsteps sounded from inside the house as someone approached. The door opened, and a woman with hair the color of cayenne pepper surveyed her with curious blue eyes. "Hello," she said.

"Hi. I'm looking for Justin Smith. Is this his place?"

The woman smiled. "Ah, yes. You must be Lyndsey."

"I am."

"I'm Solis McGuire, Justin's friend. Come on in. He's out back." She opened the door wider to allow Lyndsey to enter, then led the way through the house. "Justin found an injured owl, so he called me to see what I could do. I have somewhat of a special connection with animals."

"Like an animal whisperer?"

"Something like that," the redhead said with a gentle laugh.

Lyndsey followed Solis as she exited the house and porch, leading her into the backyard. The yard was dotted with barren trees except for a few pines that were clumps of green. A small area had been cleared of snow. Her cousin knelt beside an oversized animal cage with a huge, beautiful owl inside. Justin's left arm was wrapped with a tan towel, and he wore heavy garden gloves. He must've been trying to get the owl out of the cage.

He sat back on his heels, waving at the two women with a gloved hand. "Every time I go to grab him, he scoots to the back and pecks at me."

"Let me try," Solis said. She slipped a long leather glove over her left hand and arm as if she did this all the time. Then she knelt, reaching into the cage with her bare right hand. A stillness seemed to surround them, floating through the back porch like a breeze. She held her hand perfectly still as she coaxed the bird to her. "Come on, baby. Step up. You'll be fine."

Justin met Lyndsey's gaze with a lifted brow. "Hi," he said with a calm voice.

She smiled.

The owl eased onto Solis's wrist, and she slowly brought the bird out. She transferred it carefully as it gradually stepped along her gloved arm. Holding the animal close to her, she whispered something Lyndsey couldn't understand, nuzzling her forehead against the raptor's neck as she gently stroked its breast.

Lyndsey held her breath. If the owl turned its head, it could easily take out a chunk of Solis's cheek with its hooked beak. But it didn't. It seemed as content as could be.

Solis gently ran her hand over the bird. Checking for injury, Lyndsey guessed. She didn't want to ask since she didn't want to interrupt the magical communication between the woman and the bird.

Finally, Solis said, "I'm going to name you Spencer. You're a handsome guy." She moved toward the door. "He'll be fine. His wing may be weak for a short while, but it will heal. I'm going to take him home if he allows me to, okay?"

Justin nodded.

"You could put him back in the cage," Lyndsey suggested.

Solis shook her head. "The animals I care for choose to be with me of their own free will. I don't use cages. At least not small, confining ones like that. My larger, more dangerous animals live in huge enclosures. I use those mainly to protect the other animals."

The woman was either brave or crazy.

"I'm a photographer," Lyndsey said. "May I take your picture?"

"If that's what you're compelled to do." Solis smiled.

As Lyndsey snapped a few shots, the woman didn't pay her any attention. She was striking in her simple white sweater with her red hair braided down the back. In a calm voice, she continued to speak to Spencer. "I think you'll like my place," she said. "You can come and go as you please."

After traveling through the house with Justin and Lyndsey following, Solis paused and grinned at Justin. "Thanks for calling me. He may not have fared well on his own. The wing doesn't seem to be broken, but it's definitely injured."

"Glad you could help. He's so beautiful." Justin opened the front door for Solis.

She turned to Lyndsey. "It was nice meeting you. Enjoy your stay."

"Thanks. Nice to meet you, too." Lyndsey was still awed by the special connection Solis had with the owl.

When the door closed, Justin gave Lyndsey a giant hug, arching his back and lifting her feet off the ground. "I'm glad you could visit. It's been too long."

"Almost six years, I'd say."

"Wow. Time flies. Were the roads bad? I was worried about the snow."

"They'd been plowed, so I didn't have any trouble," she answered. "But I'll need to put on the snow chains for my return trip."

He nodded. "Well, let's get your stuff inside and settle you in."

They both traipsed outside. The taillights of Solis's vehicle winked as she tapped her brakes, then continued down the street. Lindsey rubbed her hands up and down her arms at the chill.

Her belongings included one suitcase in the trunk and the camera equipment in the backseat, along with the supplies that had tumbled onto the floor. It was too cold to leave any equipment in the car since the temperature could damage the lenses, so she made sure she took everything inside.

Justin directed Lyndsey to her room, carrying one of her suitcases. Off the living area, a short hall formed a *T*.

"The place has two bedrooms. Mine is on the left, yours the right, and we share a bathroom. I hope that's okay with you."

Lyndsey shrugged. "Just like when we were kids."

"Yep. We've never lived in mansions."

"Speaking of mansions. What can you tell me about the one around the corner? On Sleepy Hollow Way, I think. The owner's name was David."

"Thurston Mansion?"

She tilted her head. "It could be. I sort of stopped to ask for directions."

"At that estate?"

"Well, actually, the house intrigued me. I wanted to take a few pictures."

Justin grimaced. "You didn't…"

She hesitated, wondering at his reaction. But then she shot him a smile, lifting her chin. "I did. But my timing wasn't the best. He came marching out and made me stop."

"I'm not surprised. The ang—" He stopped abruptly as if catching himself. "I'm not sure how to explain this. Terror isn't like other towns. It is…old-world. It has its own hierarchy and ruling councils. The family of Thurston kind of used to run the town—like a boss family in the Mafia, I guess," he started. "Plus, the residents here are pretty fussy about their privacy. They don't take kindly to interference, and they tend to keep to themselves unless they're hanging out in town."

She raised a brow. "Sounds a bit archaic to me."

"I like the way everyone keeps to themselves." He shrugged. "Don't worry about it. You won't be here long enough to need to know any of that anyway."

"Is that why you've hidden away up here?"

He shrugged. "I haven't given it much thought." When he strolled into the kitchen, she followed. He opened the freezer. "Pizza okay for dinner?"

"Whatever is fine by me, thanks." She let the subject of David Snyder go. Something seemed off about the man. Whatever it was, her cousin knew more than he was saying. Lyndsey smiled. She loved a good mystery.

Justin fired up the gas oven, unboxed the frozen pizza, and slid the pie inside. He opened the refrigerator, then peered around the door. "Beer or soda?"

"Beer, please."

He grabbed two bottles, then popped the tops. "It's a local craft brew. Quite decent."

The kitchen filled with the aroma of the cooking pizza, and the air warmed from the heat of the oven. It felt wonderful. He set the bottles on the table.

"Can I get the plates or something?" she asked.

"Nah. Just relax. The drive can be pretty grueling when it snows."

"It wasn't bad. The roads were decent." Snagging the bottle closest to her, she took a drink. "Mmm. This is good. Smooth."

He nodded with a half-smile. "You won't find much road-clearing in town. Just the roads around town and the main street of Omen Ave." He slid plates, silverware, and a paper towel to use as a napkin in front of her.

She squinted at her cousin. He seemed different, somehow. More confident and relaxed. She hadn't seen him in a long time, so she guessed that could do it. He was an adult now, not a teen leaving home to make his mark on the world. But he seemed to carry a secretiveness that hadn't been there before.

Leaning against the stove, he returned her stare. "What made you decide to visit Terror?" he asked. "Don't get me wrong. I'm glad to see you. It's just…your call was unexpected."

Her cheeks grew warm. When he'd gone to college, they'd lost touch. "I was combing through pictures when I came across one of us at the Winter Carnival beside the enormous ice sculptures." She shrugged. "I miss those days."

He smiled, his furrowed brow smoothing. "I haven't thought about that in ages. Those were good times."

Lyndsey grinned. "When I found it, I decided there was no time like the present to get back in touch. And here I am."

Now that she thought about it, she wasn't sure what had drawn her to make this trip. The picture, sure, and the feeling that came with it had nudged her. And she usually listened to the unusual sensations she got. Had it been loneliness? Did she want to recapture the friendship they'd once shared? Or was it that he'd been the one person who had accepted her just the way she was, even with her psychic quirks?

"So where's Uncle Steve now?" he asked.

"In New York City. Dad moved there when I was in college."

He nodded. "Mine remarried. My stepmother has kids of her own. I pretty much stay in Terror." He leaned a shoulder against the doorframe. "It's not that I blame him. After our moms died and I was an adult, I just didn't have anything in common, and no history, with his new family."

"That makes sense to me." Lyndsey gave a small smile. He was still the loner he'd always been, even when they were kids. They'd grown up living a block from each other. Their mothers were sisters, and they had been close. On Sundays, they used to have cookouts in the backyard, all gathered around a picnic table.

Justin and Lyndsey had been together when they'd gotten the news their mothers had died. A church in downtown Chicago had been hosting a charity event then it had collapsed with their mothers inside. He'd been twelve and she thirteen when they came home from the movies to discover a sheriff's car in the driveway. They'd ridden their bikes because the theater was nearby.

Her father had met her on the lawn, his eyes red. He'd been crying. She couldn't recall ever seeing her father like that before.

She had shared a worried look with Justin. Then his dad had come from around the sheriff's car. Charles Smith's big hand had clasped her father's shoulder as they approached the kids. She had jumped off her bike, letting it fall on its side. The Blue Moon Wisteria had been in full bloom, and the sweet, floral scent had filled her nostrils as she took a breath. "What's wrong?" she'd asked.

Ever since that day, Lyndsey hadn't cared for the scent of the flower. She had stood there, rooted in place, waiting for the world to change. And it had. The moment her dad had told her that her mother had gone to Heaven.

"How could Mom leave me like that?" she'd cried.

Looking back, her saving grace had been that she and Justin were going through the same thing. They'd hugged each other and cried and talked and shared memories. They'd kept in touch because they shared a bond.

A tightness formed in her chest because this was the first time she'd seen him in years.

The oven timer beeped. Justin pushed the sleeves of his sweatshirt up, revealing his muscular forearms. *Geez, he had changed.* He removed the pizza, then cut it into slices. Assessing, she watched him. He was the same, yet different. Gone was any semblance of youth. In its place was a tall, strong, handsome man. There was a bit of an edge to him now, too. The town of Terror seemed to agree with him.

As he dropped a slice onto her plate, their eyes met. She blinked at his expression, noting his face was blanketed with worry. Was it because of her encounter with David Snyder?

Lyndsey hoped not. She set her camera beside her on the table as she ate. Her eyes lingered on the camera port where the memory card resided. She was looking forward to some quiet time this evening so she could look over the shots.

But then he cleared his throat and smiled, his gaze softening again. "Finish up," he said. "We're going out."

"Where?"

"The Winter Solstice Celebration and bonfire is tonight. Everyone in town will be there."

Everyone? she wondered as David's face flashed in her mind.

A little bit later, David had his coat on and was in the truck, ready to head to town. As he pulled out of the drive, his thoughts spun to that beautiful photographer from earlier. He'd liked the way she'd tipped her head and smiled, and the depths of her chocolate-brown eyes. She'd mentioned she was staying with Justin for a few weeks, and David found himself hoping he'd run into her again. He almost turned the truck around to take a drive down Norwood just to take a look-see.

He glanced in his rearview mirror as he backed out of the drive, thinking. Justin was one of the few human residents who made Terror their home. He even sat on the Paranormal Council, representing the human population. The thing about humans in Terror was they usually had some kind of supernatural calling and ancestry they didn't know about. It was why they were drawn here. If Justin had a hidden calling, Lyndsey most likely did, too. And even though he'd been aggravated by her taking pictures, he'd experienced a strong visceral connection to her at the same time. As if their paths were meant to cross again—as if her soul spoke to his.

He shook his head. Unexpectedly, his truck began to skid. *Damn ice.* He tried to steer into it to gain traction, but the patch of ice must have been a big one. The truck kept sliding. He careened off the road. The vehicle bumped over a pile of packed snow, going airborne. His head smacked into the ceiling—he never wore a seat belt. What was the point? He was immortal.

The truck landed nose-first into a snowbank. As his body rocked back and forth, his vehicle settling, he rethought the seat-belt strategy. Though he couldn't die again, it didn't mean he couldn't feel every pounding pain. Groaning, he stretched, cracking his neck.

For a long moment, he sat still, gripping the steering wheel, allowing the snow and ground to calm around him. Two thoughts raced through his head—one, he shouldn't have been thinking about Lyndsey, and two, he wasn't going to be able to get his truck out by himself.

He glanced around for his cell phone, spotting it on the corner of the passenger side floor. Trying to get his large body over the console to reach it was nearly impossible. By some miracle, he stretched far enough for his fingers to latch on to the phone.

With an exhale of air, he rested with his feet on the driver's side. Who should he call? He'd start with Diego. After he selected the number, he pushed the button to place the call.

"Hey, man. I won't make it to see the bike," he said when Diego answered. "I hit some ice, and my truck is in a snowbank."

"S'all good," Diego said. "You hurt?"

"Eh, I'm fine. Just a few bumps."

"All right, good." Diego's voice shifted, any trace of concern now gone. "I can come to pull you out."

"That would be great. You may need heavy equipment. I'm nose-first in the bank. The snow covered the front end so heavily I can't get out."

"Got it. Give me your location, and I'll be there in a few."

David gave him directions, ended the call, then tipped his head back, resting it against the passenger's side window. The sky was blue and clear. No one would ever know by looking up that the weather was a frigid twelve degrees outside. He grabbed his coffee and took a sip, his mouth tugging up. It was still hot. He tried to ration the drink, savoring its warmth for as long as he could. The temperature must have dropped ten degrees inside the cab of the truck now the heat was off.

He swiveled, navigating his legs to the passenger side. The snow appeared shallower on this side. He tried to open the truck door, but it hung up on the snow. Geez, he was in deep. Again and again, he shoved, throwing his shoulder into it.

When he heard the rumble of a tow-truck engine, he glanced over his shoulder. Diego had arrived. His friend hopped out of the vehicle, then tromped through the snow. Val Solberg, the sheriff and a fellow resident of Thurston Mansion, was a few steps behind him. They both held a shovel, which they used to dig at the snow to create an opening, freeing up outside the truck door so it would open. "I see you brought help," David said to Diego. The angel slid past the open truck door, then pushed it closed behind him.

"I was at the shop when you called," Val explained.

"Good timing, then," David said.

Together, the three assessed the situation and how they would free the truck. "You're stuck pretty deep," Diego said, shaking his head.

"Yeah. I lost control when I hit some ice."

He thumbed toward his mansion. The image of the pretty photographer flickered in his memory again.

"Wait a minute," Val said. He put a hand on David's shoulder. "I can help. You guys stand back. I may be able to melt the snow."

Since Val was a dragon shifter, he could easily create enough heat to carry out the task.

"Just don't torch my truck," David said with a laugh.

Val gave a thumbs-up.

David and Diego took their positions beside the tow truck. The areas on both sides of his Silverado were nothing but the open ground…and snow, lots of snow. The closest trees were yards away. Val stood in the clearing, shifting into his dragon form. David had seen him do it plenty of times, but every instant was a remarkable thing to behold. Val's striking scales shone in the sunshine. With every movement, they sparkled and shimmered in hues of silver and blue. Shuffling forward, he exhaled long pulses of fire at the snowbanks, melting it into a puddle of water as if it were an ice cube, leaving small clumps of snow closest to the Silverado. Steam billowed off the ground and around the truck.

"Way to go," David said as Val shifted back to his human form.

"Good to have you around, dragon." Diego removed some heavy chains from a compartment in the side of the tow truck. He attached the chains to the underside of the Silverado. "With the heavy snow gone, it will be easy to get her out." To David, he said, "Put it in neutral, then I'll pull it back onto the road."

David nodded. He climbed in, shifted into neutral, and watched Diego in the side mirror. At first, the tires spun in the icy mud. Soon, the tow truck dominated, and the Silverado began to move backward. David steered, turning the wheels until they found the pavement.

He pressed on the brakes, and the truck stopped. After he put it in park, he stepped out. "Thanks," he said.

Diego unhooked the chains. "No problem. You still gonna come check out the bike?" he asked as he put them away. Val held the compartment open as the chains clanked going in.

"Sure. And we can take a look at my truck to make sure there wasn't any damage."

"Okay. See you in a few," Diego said. "Hop in, dragon."

Solis McGuire pulled her gray Subaru Crosstrek alongside them and stopped, rolling down the passenger window. "Is everything okay?" she asked.

"It is now," David said with a smile.

"Glad to hear it," Solis said, giving him a thumbs-up. Her gaze slid to where his truck had been lodged, and the pickup-sized hole in the snowbank. "Looks like winter has begun."

She shook her head, smiled, and drove off.

David closed the door behind him, then strolled into the heart of the shop. A bike lift was positioned in the middle of the work area, but the motorcycle wasn't on it. Val stood at the front of the bike, arms crossed over his massive chest.

Off to the side. Diego propped his hip against the black-and-gray tool chest as he swiped a rag over a motorcycle part. "This isn't the season for Sunday drives. Need to drag out the snowmobiles for that. So it's a perfect time to fix this baby up."

"And this baby is?" David asked as he came closer.

"A Suzuki Intruder. Only a few things to fix up, new tire, seat, tweak the clutch, and she'll be ready to go," Diego said.

"Nice," Val said.

"Getta load of these sweet skull brake levers," Diego pointed out.

David leaned in. The skulls were an extra touch. He'd been thinking of a bike for some time. "Am I allowed to sit on it?"

"Sure."

He swung his leg over, settled onto the seat, and took hold of the handles. "I can almost feel the freedom coming off it right now." The wind in his hair, the oneness with the road. He loved his truck, but this would simply be fun.

"It's a lot like my Shadow. I had an 86 Shadow for a little bit," Diego added.

"How much?" David asked, more since it was expected than because he cared. Money was never an issue. It was one of the concerns he left behind when he died. As an angel, everything was taken care of by unseen forces. Abraham, the commander of the angels, seemed to have endless resources. There was a bank account for all the angels to use. May as well help out the locals and enjoy himself while he could.

"Thirteen hundred," Diego said with a shrug.

David nodded. "Fix it up, and I'll take it."

"Excellent. I knew you were a fit."

Val gave a throaty chuckle. "You have a gift of matching a machine and owner. So, where's mine?"

Diego sighed. "Patience, my friend. I haven't found that perfect bike for you yet."

The alarm on Val's phone dinged. He glanced at the message. "I have to pick up Twyla. See you tonight."

"Meet you at the bonfire?" David asked.

"Yeah." Val clapped a hand over his shoulder as he passed, heading for the door.

David climbed off the bike. "I better head out, too." He wished everything were this easy, including dealing with a sassy photographer. But she sure was beautiful with a certain allure about her. "Thanks, man. I look forward to spring and riding the roads."

Justin parked his truck beside the many others filling the seemingly vacant lot off Omen Avenue. Lyndsey scanned the area, then got out of the vehicle. As she shut the door behind her, she swung her camera over her shoulder. The clock tower across the street struck seven. The musical, pleasant sound contrasted with the gothic buildings and shadowed cover of the night.

She wrapped her scarf tighter around her neck. The temperature had dropped considerably, and she could see her breath with every exhale.

They walked to a grouping of tents. It was a carnival-like atmosphere with food booths selling sausages on sticks, hot cider, and funnel cakes. Wow, it had been eons since she'd indulged in one of those. She bought one. The guy handed it to her straight from the kettle, piping hot. The first bite was sugary bliss. She offered some to Justin, but he shook his head.

She looked around as she ate. People had set up their own games. In the center of the area, there was an enormous pile of wood items. Several men split logs, then tossed them on the stack. David caught her eye. Her heart did a silly skip-patter, watching as his biceps bulged when he raised and lowered the ax, easily parting the wood beneath his powerful assault. After building the mound higher, he joined another well-built man who offered him a torch. The two men swung the torches over their heads, seeming to be doing a ceremonial lighting. David was on the right. The pair interacted, posturing some ritualistic interchanges she didn't understand but enjoyed watching. She itched to pull out her camera to snap a few pictures, but she resisted. David moved with the masculine yet lethal grace of a warrior. Judging from the whoops and cheers from the crowd, the other man's name appeared to be Val.

Finally, the two men touched the ends of their torches together, then tipped them toward the dry wood and released them. The stack must have been doused with some sort of accelerant because the pile burst into flames. David and Val jumped away from the blaze with hearty shouts of success.

Justin explained the tradition. "David and Val fight against evil. Then the bonfire symbolizes the release of wishes, dreams, and fears that are passed into the fire, calling upon positive energy."

The fire quickly grew into a raging inferno.

The heat of it shocked her body, and she instinctively stepped backward. Raising her camera, she took shots of the cheering crowd. A group of four women danced. One she recognized from her cousin's house earlier today, Solis. There was also an older woman with gray-and-black hair who had a raven on her shoulder. Val scooped the forth beautiful woman with waist-length dark hair into his arms before twirling her around. She pulled his head down to kiss him.

In a flash, her camera flew from her hands.

She gasped. "What th—"

She spotted her camera in David's hand. He'd snatched it from her, the overpowering beast.

"Hey!" She plunked her hands on her hips. "Didn't your mother teach you to use your words?"

He cocked his head.

"Guess not," she grumbled. Then, more loudly, she said, "You could have *asked* me to stop taking pictures if that was what you wanted."

"I did. Besides, action is faster."

"No. You asked me not to take pictures of *your property*. We are in *public*. You can still ask me to stop, but I don't have to agree." She glared. "This is the second time you've interfered with my shots. What is it with you?"

"We don't allow paparazzi in Terror."

"I'm not a paparazzo. I'm a *photographer*."

Justin gave her a pleading look, leaning over to whisper in her ear. "Privacy, remember?"

She sighed. "Okay, I'm putting it away." She slipped the lens cap on her camera. Her cousin gave her a smile of thanks, and she forced one back.

"Thank you," David said, but it wasn't convincing.

"When a door closes, open a window," she muttered. David certainly piqued her curiosity. Maybe she should pay more attention to this small town…

He stopped short. "What did you say?"

"Huh?"

"Just a second ago."

She scrunched her brow. "You mean when a door closes, open a window?"

"Yes. I haven't heard that in a long time…"

"It's a saying my mom used a lot. Then she would go on and on about how we were saved by a stranger who shoved us out of the way of a truck when I was a little girl."

Sucking in a sharp breath, David stepped back. He was a mysterious, intriguing man.

"It's all right," she said. "It was a long time ago. I don't even remember it happening. I only remember what my mom shared with me."

His eyes darted around, looking everywhere but at her. "Sorry, I shouldn't pry."

Lyndsey nodded, focused on the fire. She hadn't thought of the incident in an exceptionally long time. Her mother had been the one who had kept alive the memory of the man who had died to save them. Goose bumps rippled over her flesh while thinking about it. She wasn't entirely sure if things happened by coincidence or fate, but she did know the person she was today was a direct result of those openings and closings. And she'd had a few doors slammed in her face so hard they had shaken her to her core. When her mother had died, that was the hardest. She missed her mom so much.

"Do you want to talk about it?" he asked.

"No." His question surprised her. Had her silence been that noticeable? Why would he even care? She glanced at Justin, who seemed distracted as he watched the women dancing. Watching Solis, she amended.

Val came over, then clapped David's shoulder. "Another year. Another fire. Want to grab some food with us?" he asked his friend, indicating the woman beside him.

Justin rotated, making quick introductions. "Lyndsey, meet Val Langdale, sheriff of Terror, and Twyla McGuire, a local florist and horticulturist. This is my cousin, Lyndsey. She'll be hanging at my place for a while."

Lyndsey nodded in greeting, offering a warm smile. "Pleased to meet you both. And Twyla, I suppose there's not much growing this time of year."

"I have a fabulous greenhouse that keeps me busy."

"McGuire? Are you related to Solis? I met her earlier at Justin's. She has a way with animals."

"Solis is my sister. Our youngest sister, Luna, and my mom, Nora, are right over there." She pointed to the still-dancing group.

"I've been watching them. They get into this."

"The entire town does," Twyla said.

David crossed his arms, then angled his head toward Lyndsey. "Have you two eaten dinner? Want to grab a bite with us?"

It was sweet of him to ask. "Yes, we have, but thank you."

He nodded. "Okay." His voice seemed to soften. "See you around." He smiled then, the firelight warming his features.

Geez, he was a handsome man. A lot of the men here could make the A list. Her gaze slid to David, and before she could start drooling, she spun around to hook her arm around Justin's. "You live in a remarkably interesting town, cuz. Just saying."

He drew her in the opposite direction of the crowd. "You don't know the half of it."

4

David followed Val without paying attention to where they were going. He was too stunned by what he'd just learned. Could Lyndsey honestly recall that incident when he'd saved her as a child all those years ago?

They headed into a burger place, then landed a table near the window as another group left. David snagged the chair that had the best view of the crowd outside. He ordered quickly at the counter, paid, and returned to his spot.

"Interested?" Val asked.

David jolted. "What?"

"The new face?"

Oh, Val was referring to Lyndsey. "Uh, no. She's not my type."

"Really?" The sheriff raised an eyebrow. "You're looking for her right now."

David shrugged. So what if he was. "Not because I'm romantically inclined. She just told me something that surprised me is all." Inhaling a deep breath, he allowed his gaze to shoot to Twyla, who was getting their order.

Val sat back in his seat, waiting for David to explain.

"I'll fill you in when I know for certain," he said instead.

Val chuckled. "Come on. Spill."

David shook his head. Thankfully, Twyla delivered their food, sliding two trays onto the table.

"Thanks for grabbing mine," David said.

"No problem. Especially since you were…preoccupied." With a smirk, she popped a fry in her mouth.

"Not you, too," David groaned.

"We're your friends," she said. "We know you whether you like it or not."

They did. As much as he'd allowed them to see who he truly was, anyway. Terror was a close-knit town; they watched out for one another. But the creatures who lived here all had hidden skeletons. When they were good, they were excellent, and when they were bad…well, all hell broke loose.

"Yes, but a man has to have some secrets," David said as he unwrapped his burger and took a bite.

Val gave him a hard look, the kind that said *we'll talk about this later*. But he dropped the subject.

David skimmed the crowd again as he hungrily ate. He easily picked out Lyndsey with her honey-brown hair and in a cream-colored parka. She was with Justin and the McGuire witches, Twyla's sisters, Solis and Luna. Since Justin lived in town and was a member of the council, he wondered how much Lyndsey knew about Terror and its residents. Given her natural smiles and reactions to the people who walked by, he guessed she didn't know much.

He finished the final bite of burger, then chased it with fries and a Coke.

He tilted his head and narrowed his eyes as he glimpsed

a man lurking in the shadows behind and to the right of Lyndsey. He seemed content to stay there, just watching. Justin and Lyndsey's group moved to chat with Diego, lion-shifter Rylan, and his wife Zoe, who was new to Terror but appeared to fit right in with the local witch coven. Shadow Man followed at a distance, stopping when Lyndsey halted. David couldn't tell for sure who the man was fixated on, but there was an odd, *off* sensation in his gut. Like the one he got when he drank milk that had soured.

Caleb? Was that the demon in human form?

His dinner churned in his stomach.

First, he'd gotten the note earlier that morning, then he'd discovered Lyndsey was the child he'd saved, and now this guy appeared to be following her. What was going on?

David leaned closer to Val. "You see the guy over there near Beauty & Beast? Do you know who he is?"

Val peered across the square at the restaurant. "Doesn't look familiar. But lots of people visit during Winter Solstice. Why?"

"Not sure yet." David stood. "But he seems interested in Justin and his group over there."

"Where Lyndsey is," Val noted.

David rolled his eyes. "Yeah. I'm going to check him out. Catch you guys later." He headed for the door.

"Hey, you're a lot of fun tonight," Val sarcastically called after him.

David waved him off. He had to find Caleb to send him on his way.

$$\mathcal{J}$$

Justin's friends seemed to have an inside joke Lyndsey *really* wasn't following. Rylan spoke of recently returning from a place called Nocturne Falls, where he'd met Zoe.

Evidently, the Georgia town celebrated Halloween all year round. She didn't know if she could live somewhere like that, but it seemed like a cool place to visit.

She thought of how St. Paul celebrated the Winter Carnival at the end of January. That was a huge deal for the area. There were legend and folklore behind it, complete with characters and tradition. Perhaps Nocturne Falls had something like that, too. She would have to check it out someday.

Right now, though, she felt very much the outsider. She burned to pick up her camera to snap some candid shots. It was a way to hide and belong at the same time. Remaining near the group, she turned her back to them. She glanced around to see if David was nearby to scold her. Nope. So she eased away from the group, raised her camera, and took shots of the fire and the crowd. She wasn't looking for anything in particular. It was fun to see what turned up when she examined her memory card. There were usually a few keepers out of the hundreds of photos.

Several people joined Justin and his friends as she stepped away and rotated, capturing a picture of the old building that was kitty-corner across the street from where she stood with the group. The moon was almost full, and the roofline of the three-story building stood out in sharp relief. It had interesting shapes with several winged statues holding hourglasses, fleur-de-lis placed along the edge the roof and at the turret on top. As she photographed it, she brought the camera down to street level. A figure stood on the far corner, staring in her direction. Then another came into the frame a bit behind him.

"Hey, you ready to go home?" Justin asked, startling her.

Her head jerked up as she cradled her camera, curling her wrist inward. "Uh, yeah. Whenever you are."

"I figured you'd be tired after the drive today," he said.

"Thanks for thinking of me. I'm doing okay, though, so whenever you're ready is fine."

His gaze swept the area. "People are leaving anyway. We can leave."

She noticed then that Solis and Luna were departing, too.

"Bye," Solis said. "See you around."

Lyndsey smiled at the redhead. "Yes. It was nice seeing you again."

As Justin led the way to his old green truck, she peered over her shoulder to the street corner. Both men were gone. She hadn't had a chance to zoom in for a closer look.

From the darkened street beside the burger place, David had allowed his wings to open. Using a glamour to camouflage himself, he flew a roundabout path to the alley beside Beauty & Beast. When he landed, he kept to the shadows. The man leaned against a light post, his back to David. He couldn't see the stranger's face or make out who he was any better than he had from across the street.

David moved slightly closer. From behind the guy, he could see Lyndsey holding her camera to her eye. Justin strolled up to her, and her gaze shifted to her cousin.

She had been taking more pictures. Had she at least capture the mystery man?

A growl formed in his throat. The man turned, and their eyes met. David blinked, stunned, witnessing pure evil in the fiend's yellow gaze. He'd seen this guy before, but it took him a moment to place when and where. *Caleb.*

The demon sprinted toward the clock tower before David could call out. Caleb disappeared into the trees on the far side. David pursued him, but the demon was crazy fast. At the tower, David halted, resting his hands on his knees, breathing hard. He stared into the darkness. The eyes and face of the guy grew clearer in his mind, and then it hit him.

Those eyes were the last thing he saw before he'd struck David with his truck that fateful night—the night he had died. *Caleb.* He'd learned the demon's name from fellow angels. His specialty was snuffing out the lives of children and causing parents the worst agony they could experience.

From the street, there was a burly rev of an engine, then the screech of tires. A truck zoomed out from between parked cars. David glanced to the left, seeing Lyndsey cross the street with her cousin. He shifted his gaze to the vehicle barreling down the road. Caleb stared straight at him, a smirk on his face.

He was going to run her down.

"Lyndsey," David called.

She didn't hear him, but she paused in the middle of the street to say something to Justin.

"Don't bother, Angel. I intend to finish what I meant to do years ago. She's mine," the demon announced with fanfare.

David's chest hurt, and fear stole his breath. No. He took one giant step forward, thrust himself into the air, and expanded his angel wings to their full sixteen-foot span. Then several things happened at once. With a powerful slice through the air, he flew to Lyndsey, grabbing hold and taking flight with her. He clipped Justin, knocking him back.

The truck barreled past, just missing Justin. David winged to the far side of the street where he released Lyndsey by a streetlamp. She fell against him, gasping for air. He looks at her. They are suddenly so close. It would be so easy to move another couple of inches, to kiss her. Her eyes seem to welcome the idea.

He hovered, brushed hair from her lovely face, and

touched his fingers to her temple, erasing the last minute or so from her memory.

Caleb stared straight at him as he rolled down the road. Son-of-a-bitch.

Since Lyndsey was okay, David continued onward to the clock tower, then pursued the truck until it came to a sudden stop in front of Misery Inn. He flew down, already running as his feet touched the ground. Coming alongside the truck, he threw open the driver's door.

Nothing. Caleb was gone.

In a haze, Lyndsey shook her head. "What just happened?" She glanced at Justin, who was getting up off the street. Had he fallen? Had too many beers? She hadn't noticed, and she held onto the light pole until a round of dizziness faded. "Are you okay?" she asked.

"Yes. The guy in the truck was in a hurry. But I'm fine. How about you?"

"I'm good. But suddenly very tired. I'm going to sleep like a rock tonight."

Back at his house, she'd said good night to Justin, dressed for bed, and yawned. Just one thing to do before melting into the mattress. She opened her laptop to transfer from her camera, then plugged the cord into the port and hit "Import." Lyndsey was OCD about one thing in her life—her pictures. Without fail, she filed them every evening by date. As the files uploaded, she washed her face and brushed her teeth.

By the time she'd returned to the bed, the download

process had completed. After finishing with her camera, she put it away and fell onto the pillow, ready to put the day behind her. Closing her eyes on a slow exhale, she let her body relax.

But thoughts and images of the bonfire, ceremony, and a hot guy by the name of David danced through her head. Her mind wouldn't shut off.

As tired—no, exhausted—as she was, Lyndsey couldn't sleep. The sound of the truck's screeching tires played in her head over and over. It tapped into a memory she shouldn't be able to recall at all, yet she did. It was a jumble of sound…a man yelling, her mother's scream, an engine barreling down on her, the odor of burning rubber, and the sharp sensation of falling.

Sitting up, she forced the recollection aside.

She grabbed her laptop, turned the pillow on its end, and plumped it so she could lean against the wall for support. The room felt cold and a bit drafty, and she wished she had another blanket. Maybe the house didn't have proper insulation. It *was* an older home. With a shiver, she tucked her legs deeper beneath the covers, resting the laptop across her thighs.

She yawned, glancing at the time clock on the screen: *12:30 AM*. She yawned again. Perhaps she'd just put the photos in a folder by location, then go to sleep. The mattress did feel rather good beneath her…

Finished with the brief organization, she set the laptop on the bedside table and turned off the lamp. She had to get some sleep.

A cold breeze floated through the room. Lyndsey tugged the covers up beneath her chin and curled onto her side, drawing up her knees. Every time she closed her eyes, she saw the man glowering at her, and then an angel flitted overhead. How crazy was that? Geez, her imagination was working overtime tonight.

She focused on her breathing, the feel of the air as it

went in and out of her nose and down through her lungs. Expanding and contracting. Concentrate. Repeat. Once more. But as soon as she stopped directing her thoughts, the images of dark evil eyes returned. Watching.

Finally, she leaned over, opened the laptop, and found a few episodes of *The Big Bang Theory* she'd had stored there. They were always good for a laugh to lighten her mood. Bonus, they were not about angels and devils, either. With the volume set low, she let the show run softly, gazing at the screen now and then and listening to it until she dozed off.

Caleb waited until she was asleep before he changed into a shadowy black form of smoke and dust, then slipped between the cracks of the window and reformed inside her room. What to do? What to do? He observed her sleeping.

Then it occurred to him how she valued her photos. It intrigued him how a picture captured a moment in time to preserve it forever. By will alone, he operated her computer, perusing her most recent cache of precious photos. He could feel how she loved them.

Some were even of him. His human form wasn't bad, with his slicked-back hair and lovely, golden tan.

Angels and devils… He smirked at the thought as he moved a copy of the picture onto a Facebook group of the same name. May as well have a bit of fun before delivering her to Lucifer.

She moaned. He stepped back, then left the same way he'd entered.

David finished breakfast, grabbed his dogs' leashes just in case he needed them, and opened the back door. The dogs dashed out into the acres of yard making up the estate. Ruby and Prissy led the way at first, running circles around Tank, in and out of the bigger dog's legs. It was a wonder the Rottweiler didn't trip. Tank sprinted ahead, then started through the trees, sniffing at the trunks and the clumps of snow as he went. The Pomeranian sisters were more interested in getting in the way and drawing Tank's attention than finding the hidden treasure of a squirrel or some other rodent.

This was the usual morning routine.

David arched his back, stretching his wings. It was the beginning of a beautiful day. On a whim, he launched upward, soaring among the few fluffy clouds, then flipped and turned, coming back down to earth. Tank dashed to David's feet, wagging his butt and the short nub of a tail.

He scrubbed his palm over the dog's head. "I know how it is, boy. It feels good to bust out once in a while."

His cell phone chimed a double-toned beep, indicating a notification. David pulled it from his pocket, glanced at the screen, and frowned. He had an app that informed him of headlines about Terror on Facebook. A picture had popped up on the *Angels and Devils* group page. There were several from last night's festivities. In fact, one was of him and Val lighting the bonfire. Nothing too revealing as far supernatural abilities went. Val wasn't in dragon form or anything. But then he moved to the last photo and enlarged the image. It was of him, hovering on angelic wings over the newest demon in town—Caleb.

David fisted his hand. He would contact the site owner to have the post taken down. He'd done it before with other pictures from Terror, although the incidents were infrequent.

Tank dug furiously at the base of a tree, and Ruby and Prissy launched into a yipping frenzy. "What are you after?" he asked the dogs, then tromped over to get them. Off to the side, Prissy nosed at a large black feather. "That's just a crow feather," he admonished. "Come on. Leave it. Let's go inside."

But the dogs wouldn't obey. The feather had them out of sorts. Finally, he picked up the two small dogs and ordered Tank to follow. Reluctantly, he did so.

They headed inside through the back door. While the dogs went directly to their water bowls, David refilled his coffee mug. He studied the picture on his phone again.

Dammit, she'd promised she wouldn't use the pictures she'd taken.

He was about to contact the website to have the photos taken down when it occurred to him that he needed to have evidence to confront her. Next, he confirmed Justin's address.

"Anything I can help you with?" his butler, Grady, asked, coming into the kitchen.

"Just see to the dogs, please. I'll be out for a while."

Grady nodded. "Certainly."

David climbed the stairs to his bedroom suite, where he showered and dressed. He paused in his massive closet to strap on his blade, a twelve-inch sheath knife with runes engraved in the hilt and down the center of the blade. It protected some immortals and devils. Given the demon in Lyndsey's picture, he might need it.

On the way out the door, he grabbed his coat from the front hall closet. He hesitated a moment, deciding whether to fly there, which would be quicker, or to take the truck. Driving wasn't his favorite, but it was more practical and much less flashy—more *human*.

As he drove, though, he realized she'd already seen him in his angel form. How could he explain his wings away? Anger bubbled to the surface. This was why he didn't trust people with cameras, or people like her in general. The citizens in Terror knew who and what he was; he kept his real nature secret only from outsiders.

He would confront her—insist she leave Terror. If she couldn't honor his request not to share photos of his town, then so be it. She could go home.

Even with the thought, a desire to get to know her argued against banishing her. Maybe she simply needed to learn about the real Terror. How would she react then? Would she think they were all monsters?

Justin's place wasn't far, maybe six miles from the mansion. He parked along the street behind her car. With his phone in hand, he marched to the front door and knocked. As an afterthought, he checked the time on his phone. Nine thirty. It wasn't that early.

David waited, but no one answered. He glanced at the vehicles in the drive. Both Justin's and Lyndsey's were parked there. How late had they stayed out last night? He knocked a third time. A ping of concern nudged him in the chest. He hadn't been the only one in the picture she'd snapped. He'd been following a demon.

He frowned. A demon in Terror...that was a huge concern.

With that, he moved to the window on the right, held his hand up, and peered inside. There weren't any lights on, and he didn't see Justin or Lyndsey. He exhaled, his tension climbing a notch.

He moved to the next window in the house. This one was smaller, probably a bedroom, and it had a black raven feather on the sill. It seemed to be a day for feathers.

He tossed it aside and repeated the look-see routine, leaning over some shrubs. Suddenly, Lyndsey shot straight up in bed and screamed.

*

What the hell was he doing peering in her window?

Once her initial shock had dissipated, it had taken her a few seconds to figure out who was there. David. His unusually streaked hair was an immediate giveaway. Air rushed from her lungs in a relieved whoosh. Last night had been so strange. She'd chalked it up to being in an unfamiliar place, but she'd had the creeps all night long, waking every hour or so.

Justin had stopped by her room a while ago to let her know he would be gone until noon, helping Solis. That was fine with Lyndsey. She had fallen back to sleep, but she'd woken still tired and cranky.

"What are you doing?" she asked aloud, jumping from the bed and trudging over to the window. "You scared me half to death."

"I'm sorry," he grumbled, seeming as confused as she was. Then he hesitated. "We have a problem. It's about your photos."

She sighed. "Again? What's with you and my photos?" Lyndsey waved him toward the front of the house, and he nodded. She went into the living room, grabbing her sweater along the way. After putting it on, she went to the front door. She threw it open, then stood defiantly in the threshold. "I told you I wouldn't use any of your damn pictures."

"I know what you said. But…" He navigated to the page that featured the photos. "I received a notice of this post this morning. Familiar?" He passed his phone to her so she could take a closer look.

"I don't know," she said, taking the phone. "I haven't looked at my shots from yesterday." But she knew pretty much what she had taken. Although, because she snapped pictures in rapid succession, there were almost always surprises in the bunch. Sometimes the unexpected revelations were the keepers.

She slid her fingers over the image to enlarge it. The photo was similar to the ones she recalled taking last night, but she knew she hadn't done anything with those pictures. This picture looked like David—but with wings. "Hmm. Someone is exceptionally good at doctoring."

She pushed the phone toward him. "I may have taken a similar photo, but I didn't post or share it. I swear." She stared into his hazel eyes with sincerity.

He nodded. "I want to believe you. However, someone posted these pictures online."

"I don't know who it was, but it wasn't me." She stepped back, allowing him to enter the room. "Come on in. I'll get my laptop and show you what I took yesterday."

His eyebrows rose as if surprised by her invitation. "Thank you," he said. "I have grave concerns about this, for reasons we need to discuss."

She held her palm out to the living area. "Have a seat, and I'll be with you after I change." When she reached the bedroom, she glanced back over her shoulder. "Make yourself at home. There is probably something to drink in the refrigerator. I'm sure Justin won't mind."

At least, she *thought* Justin would be a good host. He was easygoing that way. Pausing on the other side of the door, she let her heart rate slow. Energy coursed through every part of her. The problem was, she couldn't tell if it was because of the surprising morning or David Snyder's presence. Every time she took stock, her pulse raced and she felt warm, even when she was freezing from the wintry weather. Why was that?

She slipped into a pair of jeans, then layered on a shirt and sweater.

The house still seemed cold to her.

She scrolled to the top of the page, and shots of the gothic mansion rolled over the screen. Then she came to the ones with David and Rylan in the frame.

That's strange…

Rylan was clear, but David's image was blurry. She scanned the other pictures of him. All were out of focus and unclear. She blew out a frustrated breath, scrolling through more of the same. What was the deal? She wasn't a sloppy photographer.

She skipped over images until she came to the ones she'd taken last evening. Some shots of lighting the fire, but the glow in the background didn't make for a good chance to see David, anyway. Then there were some of him and Val up close. Again, David was blurry.

Lyndsey pursed her lips, still glancing between the pictures. She'd always had a special connection with her photographs. It seemed she usually captured almost otherworldly elements. That was the only way she could describe it, which might be what made her photos so appealing. Glimpsing moments before or after events, experiencing how it felt in those moments—that was what she tried to achieve for her audience.

She moved to the final few shots. David filled the frame, a set of glorious wings of white-and-gold expanding behind him. She inhaled sharply. He was in midair, in mid-*flight*, and he looked like…like an *angel*. He was magnificent. The photo of him was crisp and clear, unlike all the others she'd taken of him.

Behold the truth. She blinked. This was crazy.

A few frames later, she'd captured a man beside the streetlight, glaring at David. David's brows almost touched from his intense scowl. She could practically see the anger wafting off his shoulders like steam on a hot road in summer. In the next shot, the same man faced the camera full-on. Lyndsey gasped, her entire body feeling suddenly weak. She'd seen that man before. A long time ago when she'd been a child.

Her roiling stomach sank to her toes with a memory she couldn't quite bring to her consciousness. Lyndsey had known back then she hadn't liked the man. She liked him even less now.

But why was he following David? What did he know of this man?

She eased the laptop lid down. There were so many things about Terror she didn't understand. Why she'd felt compelled to visit was at the top of her list. Yes, she enjoyed seeing Justin. It had been far too long, but there was something more to it, something she couldn't explain. That inner guide had been with her entire life, and it had drawn her to Terror.

As soon as Lyndsey went into the bedroom, he stood and paced. He was getting mixed signals from his head and his gut. She seemed to be telling the truth, yet the evidence said differently.

And Jesus… When she'd come to the door with a sweater covering her PJs, that was the sexiest thing he'd seen in a long time. The PJs looked like an oversized shirt…buttons up the front, pale green, with a curved hem that stopped slightly above her knees. She had lovely legs, and a vibrant blue sweater clung to her body to below her hips. Bare feet peeked out farther down, showing her pink polished toes. Ugh, he shouldn't be getting so worked up over her.

But he was.

David blew out a ragged breath. He wanted to draw her into his arms and hold her. Maybe kiss her. And, at the same time, he felt compelled to protect her. If she were the child he'd saved all those years ago, what did it mean that she was here now? At the same time as that demon, no less…

His steps quickened as he turned and walked around to the seating arrangement in the kitchen. The bedroom door opened, and she came into the room carrying her laptop.

He'd been wrong earlier. She looked sexy as hell this minute in her ripped-at-the-knees jeans and tan sweater, still barefoot. He cleared his throat, trying not to think about her like that.

"Did you get something to drink?" she asked.

"No."

In the kitchen, she placed the laptop on the table, walked to the refrigerator, and opened it. She leaned in, looking around. "I see water, milk, Coke, and beer. Although it's too early for beer, right? Any of that interest you? Or I can make coffee."

"Water is fine, thanks."

She plucked a water and a Coke bottle from inside, closed the door with her elbow, and faced him. "Here you go."

He took the water she held out. From where he stood, her scent wafted to him, a mixture of flowers and smoke from last night's bonfire. She hadn't showered, he surmised. Of course, he *had* woken her just moments ago, so duh. Her scent was a delicious mixture anyway, and he had to resist the urge to move closer to her.

She walked to the table, eased into a chair, and opened the laptop. Then took a long drink of soda, tipping her head back and showing her slim throat working as she swallowed. He glanced away, into the living room. "Come closer, and I'll show you the stuff I took last night."

He took a sip of his water, then did as she suggested, taking the seat next to her.

She tapped the keys a few times. "Here you go." After another gulp of Coke, she moaned. "Mmm. Caffeine."

"Don't you drink coffee?"

"Sure, but this is just as good in a pinch. I don't have to make it or wait for it to brew, so it gets into my system sooner.

"Here, I set it up as a slideshow. It will flip through every shot I took." She sat back, folded her arms over her chest, and let the images fill the screen.

David leaned forward. He had to admit she was a good sport about this. It didn't change the fact that a photo of him in his true form had been posted, but now he'd addressed it with her, he could have it taken down.

She had captured some good shots of his house and grounds—some close-ups of the birds and one of a tree with almost-bare branches had the sun peeking behind them in a sparkle of light. Then there were the ones of the bonfire with him and Val lighting the tinder. And finally, the one with that crazy demon frozen at the end of the show.

"I have a few questions that need answering, too," she said. "You know, you're not very photogenic."

"Thanks a lot," he said sarcastically.

She rolled her eyes. "You're blurry in every shot. But I'm a professional. I don't make many mistakes with my camera, not like that." She paused, angling her head at the computer screen. He said nothing. "Why do you think that is? Do you have some voodoo mojo going on?" Then she tapped the cursor to one of the final, clear images of him.

"Or could it have something to do with those wings?"

He swallowed. "I'm not here to talk about me. I only want to know how that picture got online and that it won't happen again."

"Oh, that's all?"

"Yes."

She quirked a brow. "Don't angels get in trouble for lying or something?"

He scooted his chair away from her. "You're talking crazy."

She shook her head. "Ever since I was a child and survived a near-death experience, I've had a special gift. I see true things in pictures. Things other people don't see. Like angel wings that may not show up to the regular human eyes."

"You've always had this?"

"As long as I can remember."

Perhaps that was why she had come to Terror—her bit of supernatural talent.

"Regardless, you took the pictures, and now they're on the web. What am I supposed to think about that?"

"That someone else also took pictures."

He held his phone alongside the computer screen. "You tell me. It looks like the same shot."

She leaned in, glancing between the two images. "I admit, it does. I only know I didn't put it there."

"What about Justin? Do you think he did it?"

Her brow furrowed. "No. Why would he?"

"Beats me."

"I can only say I had a tough time sleeping last night, even though I was exhausted. I just had this creepy feeling all night long, like someone was watching me."

David finished the last of his water. "In this town, you never know what's waiting around the next corner. We have more than our share of uncommon citizens. The creepy vibes may have been from that."

"I don't know," she said. "So far, I've liked everyone I've met."

He nodded. Judging from her smile, she was a good person: warm, friendly, helpful—the kind of person worth giving his life for all those years ago.

Lyndsey looked at him straight in the eye. "Tell me more about what's going on here."

7

David scanned the kitchen, trying to decide what and how much to share with her. "I need to be completely honest with you. We've met before."

"Um, I don't think so. You're kind of a memorable guy." She chuckled.

"In a good way, I hope."

"Oh, yeah. In a very good way." Her voice turned throaty, then she cleared it as if she'd said something she hadn't meant to.

He glanced at her from beneath his lashes. "It was when you were young. I'm the man who pushed your stroller out of the way of a truck—saved you and your mother."

She tilted her head, staring at him in disbelief. "But... that man died."

He held her gaze and said nothing, allowing the entire story to sink in and for her to put the pieces together. It didn't take long. She brought her fingers to her lips, her mouth dropping open. "The wings in the photo... You're an angel?" she asked incredulously. "No. No. That's not possible. Wings can be faked. It was some sort of shadow from the bonfire. Angels on earth can't be real."

He smiled slowly. "Yes. Your pictures don't lie."

"But you died for my mother and me. How…how can I ever repay you?" She turned her body, leaning into him more.

"Don't use the pictures of Terror," he said, his serious nature returning.

Her lips thinned as her brows dipped. She straightened in her chair. "I already gave you my word on that." She started to cross her arms, but then stopped. "Oh. You're joking." She laughed.

He nodded. "I don't require anything from you. But we do have a problem—one even bigger than these pictures circulating." He pointed to the other man in the photo. "This guy is a demon, the same one who tried to run you down all those years ago."

"What? Demons and angels? I can't believe it. You've got to be kidding me," she added.

"I assure you I'm not."

She shook her head. "I've found weird things in my pictures, auras, ghosts, images that foretold odd occurrences. But this…" She stared at the picture of him and Caleb on her computer screen, disbelief written on her face.

"I don't know for sure, but I'm wondering if he's here to finish what he started."

"What do you mean by that?"

"We can't discount that he may try to kill you again."

"Why? What's his interest in me? Or for my mom all those years ago?"

"I don't know."

"My mom already died." She paused, then sucked in a gulp of air. "Hey, can you check on her or anything? You know, on the other side."

"I'll see what I can do."

"That would be great." She rested her hand on top of his, where he leaned on the table. "How does your angel thing work?"

"I spend my time on earth. My assignment is to watch over Terror and its residents."

"Does everyone in Terror know what you are?"

"All supernatural beings do."

She laughed shakily. "What is this? A paranormal town out of a romance book?"

He peered at her. "It could be."

She gasped. "With vampires and shifters and witches and…and…what else?"

"That's enough, to begin with," he said. "Does that scare you?"

"Of course it does! I don't want to be eaten or to become a cocktail."

"You won't. We live by rules."

She nibbled on her lip. "Wait, you have a sheriff—Val." She jumped with unease-laced excitement laced. "Does that mean he's a supernatural being, too?"

"Val?"

"Yes."

David hesitated. He was telling her too much too fast.

"Please tell me," she coaxed.

"Val is a dragon shifter. Very dedicated. Loyal. Extremely dangerous," he said sternly. "And my best friend."

"Oh my. I can't wait to go to town. I want to meet everyone again. See them in a new light. See if I can guess their paranormal nature."

She certainly liked to live life on the edge, he thought. "Lyndsey, this isn't a game. It's who we are. It's what Terror is supposed to protect."

Her smiled dimmed. "Yes. You're right. Sorry, I got overexcited."

"Now, back to our problem…"

"It was just an accident, not an intentional attempt to

kill my mom and me. Why do you think he is after me again after all of these years?"

"Demons rarely do anything unless it will benefit them. I can only guess. One, he doesn't like losing, and he hates unfinished business. And two, he's been somewhere that he couldn't reach you." And there was the note he'd received. He didn't mention that.

"Then I'm glad I came to Terror when I did. I've always suspected there were things I couldn't explain out there, creatures who lived on the edges of reality, in the shadows. I've had this sixth sense my entire life."

"Your gifts may be why the demon targeted you."

She searched his eyes. "Does Justin know all this?"

"Yes. He's the human on our Paranormal Council. Like you, he has an element of supernatural about him. He just doesn't realize it yet. All the humans drawn to Terror seem to."

She nodded. "I don't believe a demon is after me."

"Yet, you accept I'm an angel?"

She shrugged. "My photos say it's so."

"Ah, you're telling me you can only believe what you can see?"

"Maybe. So now what do we do?

He turned his hand over, lacing his fingers in hers as he urged her to stand. His fingers moved along hers. It was the slightest touch imaginable. All he could concentrate on was the square inch of skin where they came together. "We wait." He watched her, feeling far more than he should.

Up until now, he'd considered his fate just. He didn't have a life in the traditional sense, but what he had was good enough. He'd lived his life locked away in his perfect home with his dogs and impeccable environment. And he'd told himself it was everything he'd ever wanted. But that had been a lie. What he wanted was standing right in front of him: a chance at love, the opportunity to have a messy, unpredictable, chaotic life of mystery and joy.

Lyndsey dropped into her chair, reluctantly letting go of him, releasing the delicious connection they'd shared. She leaned back in her seat to process everything David had told her. Even though it was terrifying to think that all the creatures she'd read about were real, at the same time, a sense of relief came over her. Throughout her life, she'd had this ability to see beyond what everyone else did. That emotions had colors and auroras. That sometimes, the picture revealed to her what had happened in the past or what would happen in the future. Now she knew it was real, and that it was okay.

A screech of tires stopping abruptly sounded out front. Lyndsey turned her head toward the window. "What was that?"

"Justin in a hurry?" David guessed.

"He doesn't have his truck."

Before David had a chance to respond, the front door burst open. Justin rushed inside with long, lanky strides. "I stopped by to get my cages. Somehow, all the animals got loose at Solis's place. She needs help rounding them up."

David stood. "I can help."

"I'll come, too," Lyndsey added. "Let me get my shoes and a jacket."

When she returned to the living room, she also had her camera strapped over her shoulder. David was waiting, holding open the door for her. He gave her a stern look when he saw the camera.

She shrugged. "It's what I do."

He sighed.

Justin dropped a set of cages at the door.

David carried the birdcages out to the Silverado, then set them in the flatbed. "You can ride with me," he said to Lyndsey. Justin loaded several cages into Solis's SUV, which he had borrowed since he'd left his at home.

"Okay." She trailed him to his truck, then climbed in.

They followed Justin as he pulled out of the driveway. Along the way, they passed several vehicles, all seeming to head the same direction they were. "There's a lot of people out this morning."

"Word has spread, and people are coming out to help."

"That's nice."

When they arrived, Lyndsey looked around in awe. Solis's place was an animal refuge made up of oversized pens to separate and protect the animals, yet not to confine them. It was a bigger operation than Lyndsey had imagined. Solis took in injured and stranded animals of all sorts.

David parked his truck, climbed out, and grabbed the cages from the bed. "What happened?" he asked Solis.

Smoothing her riot of red hair back with both hands, she took a huge breath. "The pens were opened. Someone did this intentionally," she said, her voice flustered, angry, and hurt.

"I may have a suspect on that." David nodded at Val, who had just walked up. "I'll explain when we're finished."

Did he mean the demon?

With a nod, Val grabbed a cage.

"I'm most worried about the big cats," Solis explained. "There's a jaguar—not native to the area—but someone got it as a kitten and couldn't keep it when she got too big. And then there's a mountain lion. I've already lost four animals to the two cats. They're in panic mode." She dipped her head at Val. "I have tranquilizers if we need them."

"Good," Val said.

She glanced at the group, then drew David and Val aside. Lyndsey strained to hear as Solis spoke. "What if you approached them by air? Maybe you could herd them back into a secure area, and we would handle it on land from there?"

David nodded his agreement. He turned to Lyndsey. "I'll be back shortly. While I'm gone, you stay with the group, understand? Don't go off by yourself."

"All right." She touched his shoulder, wanting to tell him to be careful, but she held back. They didn't have any sort of real relationship, but she knew she was growing closer to him already, that the bond between them was strengthening.

Along with the other volunteers, she watched the two men head to the backyard. David opened wings that were suddenly visible to her—he possessed the ability to hide them—and took off in flight. She had been watching David, so she missed seeing Val change into his dragon form. The next thing she knew, Val and David were doing air acrobatics over the animal compound. They circled several times. David pointed, shouting at Val. They worked well as a team, flying low and chasing the jaguar across the vast yard, right toward Solis and the enclosures.

David could follow the jaguar right to the ground, then run along after it. His wings acted like a broom, pushing it into the penned area. Solis shut the gate. "One more to go," she shouted.

David took off again to meet up with Val in the air. The mountain lion would be more difficult to spot than the jaguar; its coloring would blend in with the terrain. But with the snow on the ground, it was easy to follow the animal tracks. He signaled Val to crisscross over the area. There was only a small section of woods. Perhaps the cat had hidden there.

He dropped to the ground, going on foot into the trees and brush. Val would continue searching above. When there were open spots, David flew through the trees until they were too close together to navigate, then he'd walk again.

He approached the center of the thatch of trees, and that was when David spotted him—the demon Caleb sitting on a large slab of granite, the mountain lion at his side. He stroked the big cat from its ears to its shoulders. "Lose something?" Caleb sneered.

"Go back to Hell," David said.

"You know, I've been trying to do just that. Unlike most people, it suits me." His gaze darkened even more. "But thanks to you, I got sent to Purgatory instead."

David folded his wings against his back. "Anything I can do to help expedite your return trip?"

Caleb stroked the cat again. "As a matter of fact, there is. Give me the female."

David laughed. "Not going to happen. So you may as well just be on your way."

Caleb shook his head. "That's not how it works. You see, Lucifer won't allow me entry without making this right. I was to deliver Lyndsey and her mother twenty-five years ago, but you ruined that with your heroics. I can't believe you died for them."

"Some of us have honor; some are sorry SOBs." David crossed his arms. "Hit the road, Jack."

The tempo and angle of Caleb's strokes over the cat changed. His fingers caressed the fur beneath the animal's chin and along its throat. Murder lit his eyes. David reached for his blade and smoothly withdrew it, keeping it close to his leg. Could he fly the distance to the demon before he snapped the cat's neck? He spread his wings, then flew toward the beast.

"You beat me once," Caleb said. "I won't let that happen again. I'm ready now, and she will be mine this time."

In less than a heartbeat, the demon's fingers closed on the animal's jaw. David surged forward, raising his weapon. The blade elongated into a sword, and fire shot from its tip.

Caleb cackled as he disappeared in a swirl of black smoke, untouched.

David landed on the rock where he'd been. He dipped his head, staring down at the mountain lion. The cat rolled over, purring, paws in the air. With a long sigh, David sheathed his weapon and bent to pick up the mountain lion. "You're heavy," he moaned, then adjusted the cat's weight in his arms. He flew in spurts, walked, and flew again as the terrain allowed, backtracking the way he'd entered the woods.

Val met him in the yard as David handed the cat over to Solis. "Thank you," she said. "I doubt I would have gotten her home without your help."

"You're welcome. How are you doing with the birds and other animals?" David asked.

"We're slowly gathering them. If they're healthy enough, I'm not worried about them."

David nodded, then turned and clapped a hand on Val's shoulder. "We need to talk."

Relief weakened David's knees when Lyndsey rounded the corner. Part of him feared Caleb would find a way to get to her. Without thinking about the right or wrong of it, he drew her into his arms and kissed her head. "I'm glad you're safe."

He set her from him, gazing into her eyes. "You got the cats?" she asked.

"Yes.

"Good. I knew you would." She rested her hand on his arm.

When he felt the light pressure of her fingers, his muscles tensed. "If the animals are gathered, we can leave as soon as I speak to Val for a moment."

"Okay. I'm going to say bye to Twyla and Luna. They were at the bonfire, but I just met them. They're nice."

He let her go, watching her walk away as Val strolled over. As sheriff, Val needed to know what was going on in town.

"What's up?" Val asked.

"Solis was correct about someone releasing the animals," David said. "It was a demon by the name of Caleb. He had the mountain lion in the woods. Probably would have killed her if I hadn't drawn my sword."

"Another effing demon. We can't catch a break."

"There's more…" David sighed. "I had a run-in with him twenty-five years ago. He was driving the truck the night I was hit."

Val's eyes widened. "Wait. He *killed* you?"

"Yes. And I saved *her*." David jutted his chin toward Lyndsey.

"Unbelievable. And you don't find it suspicious they're both in town at the same time?" Val questioned.

"Darn straight, I do." He watched Lyndsey smile and

hug Luna. "Anyway, I thought you should know Caleb is here. I believe he's going to try to take her again. Evidently, he's spent the last twenty-five years in Purgatory and isn't too happy about it."

"What can I do to help?"

David shrugged. "Just let me kill the bastard if I get a chance. And keep your eyes open—he could take revenge on the town. Most likely, he'll take his wrath out on Lyndsey and me, but you never know. He's already involved Solis in this mess. There's no way to know what else he'll do or even what he is capable of."

Val seemed to consider that information. "I think I should round up a combat team to ready themselves, just in case."

"It probably wouldn't hurt," David admitted.

It was shortly before sunset when David escorted Lyndsey to the door of Justin's place. The sky glimmered dark purplish gray with peachy wisps of clouds. Night came early this time of year. "You know it was Caleb who let the animals out, right?" he said.

Her brow furrowed. "How do you know that?"

"I ran into him in the woods."

"And?"

"I don't know if I should tell you."

She shrugged. "Why not?"

"He's cruel and evil. He would have killed the mountain lion if I hadn't challenged him."

"I think he's taunting me. He may have even been here last night. That terrifies me."

"You could be right. And it's healthy to be frightened. Demons enjoy wreaking havoc before they grab their victim."

"Aren't angels stronger than demons?" she asked. She faced him, stepping close enough they breathed the same air.

"I'd like to think so. Good triumphing over evil and all that. But…not always."

"He did this to you…" She smoothed her palms over both his shoulders, then ran them down his arms to his wrists, then interlaced her fingers with his.

"Technically, a dump truck made me what I am today," he clarified. "I wasn't an angel at the time."

"True." She appeared thoughtful.

"What are you thinking?"

"Wondering how long it will be until Justin comes home. I'm not usually squeamish about staying alone. But tonight…want to sleep on my couch?" she asked. It sounded like a joke, yet there was something else in her voice. She was afraid, and he couldn't blame her.

"I'm not sure what Justin would think about that. Besides, it's not bedtime."

"All these years, I didn't know about him, so I wasn't frightened. But now…" She shivered.

"I'm sorry." He drew her closer, then pressed his lips to her brow.

"That feels good," she whispered.

He let his mouth dip lower, brushing her cheek. Then lower still until he found her lips. Gently, ready to release her at the slightest hint of resistance, he kissed her. And she reciprocated, deepening the kiss until they both moaned with desire. Slowly, she drew back and looked into his eyes. He swallowed.

"You know what? I'm hungry," he said, pulling away. "Would you like to see some of the town? I'll take you to dinner and show you around."

"Sure. Let me text Justin and see what he has planned. And I'd like to take a quick shower." Blushing, she hurried to explain. "I went to bed late, then got up late this morning."

"Whatever you want to do is fine. I'm just your bodyguard."

"Yeah." She gave a throaty laugh. "Right."

"No, seriously," he pressed. "Until we get rid of Caleb once and for all, I'm here for you. I gave my life for you once; I'm not going to let anything happen to you now."

Lyndsey felt the blood drain from her face. With every word he spoke, her guilt dug deeper. If it hadn't been for her, he would have lived. What kind of life would he have had? A wife? Children? Grandchildren?

The muscles in her face tightened as her mouth turned down.

"Hey. Hey." He cupped her cheek in his large hand. "It's okay. I would do it again. And I'd do it for anyone else, too, because that's who I am."

She nodded slowly. It was the man—correction, *angel*— she was growing to like a lot.

She enjoyed being with him. Was it possible to love an angel? Whoa, where did that come from? She was jumping way ahead of herself. But was it possible for someone to have a life with one? He seemed so human. She could touch him, hold him, and kiss him. Her tummy did a delightful jump, her emotions being tugged in different directions.

And gawd, was he a great kisser.

"Go get ready, and we'll head to dinner," he said.

"Help yourself to something to drink while you wait. I won't be long." She turned, then strolled into the bedroom. Lyndsey selected black jeans, a peach sweater, and soft leather boots with a slight heel. She carried everything, along with her toiletries, into the shared bathroom.

Twenty minutes later, she emerged, refreshed, ready to forget about demons and have some fun.

"You look fantastic," he said, his voice warm and appreciative.

"Thanks."

At the door, he helped her into her coat. "Hey, how about if we change the plan and eat at my place?"

"At the mansion?" Not that they'd had any definite plans, to begin with.

"Yes. My butler, Grady, is a terrific cook."

"That's fine. A little more peace and quiet will be nice. We've been with the townsfolk all day."

"Excellent. I'll call ahead to give Grady a heads-up. You're in for a treat. He's a fabulous cook. We can eat dinner, and then, if you still want to go into town, we can meet with a group for drinks. I can invite Justin, too, if you want."

"That sounds perfect."

David escorted her through the massive entry and central hall of the mansion. She took in the place as she went.

"The house is even more beautiful on the inside than on the outside. And great taste in art, by the way," she said, indicating the series of abstracts spaced out along the hallway.

"Thanks."

She paused, turning in a circle, taking in the three-story ceiling and the huge, open spiral staircase. "This is a lot of house for one man," she said.

"I'm not the only one who lives here. Thurston Manor belongs to the Angel Alliance. Five of us live here."

She whipped around, her eyes boring into him. "There are more of you?"

A rumble rolled through his chest. "There is only one of *me*. But four other angels, yes." He didn't think it was a good idea to mention that a dragon shifter, Trevor Kirk, also lived here in the west wing. Val used to hang here, but since his relationship with Twyla, he'd been staying at her place.

"Is Grady an angel?" she asked as the thought seemed to come to her.

"No." He extended his hand, directing her to the back of the house and the kitchen.

Grady was at the stove, fussing over the meal he was preparing.

"What would you like to drink? Wine?" David asked.

Her face lit. "Wine sounds wonderful."

He moved to show a wine cellar of sorts behind him. It was an alcove lined with stones set in the wall. Most likely, it was temperature-controlled based on the shelf level and type of wine. Reds were housed at the top with whites at the bottom for cooler temperatures. Of course, this was simply an intermediary location; a full wine cellar was located in the basement.

"Red, white, or rosé?" he asked.

"Red. But not too dry, please."

He selected one, opened the bottle, then poured her a glass. His fingers touched hers as he handed it over to her. "Do you mind if I freshen up while dinner is finishing? Grady will keep you company."

"Of course. You don't have to worry about me. I'll just sit here until I find out all of Grady's cooking secrets. You said he's a great cook." She glanced at Grady.

"Good luck with that," he said with a chuckle. "I'll be back in a few minutes. If you need anything, Grady will be happy to get it for you."

She reached across the table, then placed her hand on top of his. "Thank you."

When she touched him like that, he didn't want to leave. "No problem." Begrudgingly, he pivoted and made his way upstairs to his bedroom suite as his chest tightened. His pulse ticked up. She did that to him. But he had no right to desire her or want to make her his.

A relationship would never work for them. There were too many obstacles to overcome. He wasn't even alive!

He quickly and efficiently cleaned himself up, washing away not only the lingering odor of the demon, but also Lyndsey's sweet scent. He forced himself to turn his thoughts to the matter at hand, to why they were at his home.

While she'd been getting ready earlier, he'd been busy rethinking her situation. He'd decided the safest course for her was to stick close. First, they'd have a quiet dinner. Grady would work his magic and prepare a meal for them. Then, after dinner, they would go to Fortune's Pub, a bar next to Misery Inn. He'd already texted members of the council, plus some other friends, letting them know of the meet-up and the reason behind it. Hopefully, there would be a good turnout. They would all protect her. It would allow him to focus on coming up with a plan to get rid of Caleb for good, and she was a vulnerable mortal. No other scenario would allow for Lyndsey to have a safe, happy, and carefree life.

A knock sounded at the double doors to his suite. Grady inched the doors apart, enough to be heard inside. "Sir, dinner is ready."

Had he been in his room that long? He glanced at the clock. No. Grady had simply been extremely efficient as usual. He liked that about the man. Plus, he'd never met anyone as organized. "I'll be right there," David said.

When he entered the kitchen a few minutes later, Grady directed him to the dinette table beside the large bay window. Lyndsey was already seated, sipping what he assumed was another glass of wine. "I chose the dinette, sir, because the snow looks so beautiful."

David nodded. "Excellent, Grady. It's perfect." He took the seat across from Lyndsey, then poured wine in his glass. "More?" he asked, tilting the bottle in her direction.

"No, thank you."

Grady slid two plates onto the table. "Prosciutto-wrapped chicken breast with fontina and pasta," he announced.

"Mmm… It smells delicious," Lyndsey said.

"You outdid yourself, Grady, especially on such short notice."

Grady chuckled. "Not so. I always have something in the refrigerator ready to fix. In this household, how could I not?"

"True. But still, you amaze me. Thank you," David added. "Dig in," he suggested to Lyndsey. He ate a bite of chicken and pasta, letting his eyes roll heavenward as the flavors washed over his tongue. After he kissed the tips of his fingers, he opened them like a flower. "Magnificent."

Grady grinned, then returned to the kitchen. "I'm glad you like it."

"I can see why you enjoy your life here," she said with a hint of a smile. "You're quite spoiled." Teasingly, she raised an eyebrow.

"I am. We lack for nothing, and I enjoy Terror. I like my friends. We are a family. You'll see."

She gazed across the table at him. "I wasn't planning on staying if that's what you mean."

Noncommittally, he shrugged. He hadn't thought about her leaving. That would complicate things even more. "I meant that you just arrived."

"I know. And look at all the excitement I've had already."

They both smiled before digging into their food. "You mentioned you were a freelance photographer. Have you always done that?"

"Yes. I studied photography in college, and I began selling my work then. I also shot for a newspaper for several years, but that wasn't for me. Too structured and confining."

"Structure is my friend," he said.

"I can tell. What did you do before…" She waved her fork.

He raised his brows. "Oh, you mean before I became an angel?"

"Yes. That."

"I was an accountant."

She wrinkled her pretty nose. "Not my idea of fun."

"It was work, not fun. But I still liked it. I enjoy spreadsheets and statistics. When you put in the right information, the right numbers, you can trust the results."

"Where's the creativity and adventure in that?" She lifted her wineglass, peering over the rim at him with her big brown eyes.

"Not everyone is as creative and as adventurous as you are. I'm just a simple man."

"You are an angel. That's not so simple."

"You're right."

She nibbled on her lip for a moment. "Did you hate me or my mother for what happened to you?"

"No. Not for a second. There were other forces at work. I learned the driver was a demon." He scraped the last morsel from his plate and finished it. "Him, I can't forgive."

Her silverware dropped from her fingers, rattling on her plate. "Now we're talking demons? I can't believe it."

He held his hands open. "If there are angels, then there are demons."

She swallowed, seeming to keep her last morsel from making a reappearance. "I hadn't given that any thought." She toyed with the silverware, positioning the knife and fork neatly on her plate. "I can't eat another bite. It was delicious."

Like that, she dropped the subject of demons. He couldn't blame her. "Tank and the girls will be happy you have a light appetite."

"Who?" she asked, confusion sweeping her face.

He laughed. "My dogs."

She smiled, then took another sip of wine. "I haven't seen them."

"They stay in the den most of the time. That way, they don't bother other people and visitors." Speaking of visitors… "I'd like you and Justin to stay here until we get rid of Caleb. I worry about your safety."

She tilted her head, her lips turning up at one side.

"Both of you," he hurried on. "Humans are more vulnerable than supernatural creatures. You don't have the same defenses. If a demon is dangerous to paranormal beings, he is lethal to humans."

Swallowing, she scooted her chair back. "We'll see what Justin thinks."

"Fair enough," he said. But he wasn't concerned. He was sure her cousin would see reason.

A great benefit of having a lifeless body was he could take any shape he chose: a rock, a mouse, a man. A raven was one of his favorites. Not only did he blend in with the many ravens in Terror, but he also liked flying. And they had damn good eyesight.

He sat on a telephone wire overlooking Thurston Mansion, alongside several other ravens. Lyndsey had gone into the house with David. He was becoming more and more a thorn in Caleb's side. It seemed the angel had taken it upon himself to watch over the woman.

Eventually, though, he would make a mistake. And Caleb would be ready for it.

They always misjudged his capabilities. There weren't many creatures who truly understood demons. Witches were the closest, but angels? Their thought processes were too…nice.

He'd be able to take the girl to Lucifer soon.

After dinner, David drove her into town to experience Terror up close and personal. Fortune's was a lively pub set in the middle of the block within the Misery Hotel. They joined Diego and Justin, who had already grabbed a table sizable enough to accommodate friends. It wasn't near the fire, though, which she would have liked, but heat drifted over to her, warming her from the chill outside.

"I'll take another beer, Barbarella," Diego called to the waitress.

Lyndsey removed her coat, then sat back as several of David's friends joined them.

Looping an arm around David's, she tugged him closer. She pressed her lips to his ear, whispering. "What kind of creature is he?"

"Wolf shifter," David said softly.

Diego angled his body closer. "I can hear you," he said in a sing-song tone, then added, "Leader of the pack, at your service."

"Oh." Her cheeks heated. "Sorry. I meant no disrespect. This is all very new to me." She sat up straighter.

"Got it, sweetie." Diego took a long drink of his beer.

"And the waitress?" she said softly to David again. "She seems different, too."

"Neko Demi-Cat."

Lyndsey made a mental note to look that up when she got a chance.

Diego nodded his dark head. He clapped one hand against the other. "Okay, let's take on this demon," he shouted so everyone in their group of nine could hear. No doubt, most of the people in the next room could hear him, too. He was an enthusiastic guy who seemed to live life on the edge. He owned a motorcycle repair shop.

"Okay, I think everyone is here who could make it," David said, giving Diego a warning look. "When a demon enters our town, everyone is at risk. No matter whom he's after."

Nathaniel Newburg smirked, showing his fangs. "I know this won't be a popular suggestion, but the demon is after Lyndsey… If she leaves town, that will solve our problem."

David glared at the vampire. "Demons anywhere are our problem because they will eventually end up here." He glanced around the table, meeting everyone's gaze. "I invited you here to inform you and place you on alert. No sense getting the entire town in a panic, but we should be prepared."

"He's already caused trouble for Solis and her animals," Val said.

Nora, the matriarch of the McGuire family, nodded, then flipped her black-and-gray hair from over her eyes. "Let me remind you of some things about demons. Many times, you don't know they're even present. They can possess objects and animals, turn brother against brother. And they have no morals. They consider what they do a game."

"How do we stop them, then?" Lyndsey asked.

"You trick them. And kill them face to face," Nora replied.

"Sometimes, they're not as smart as they think they are," Diego chimed in.

"But sometimes, they *are*," David stressed. "It helps to be aware and watchful. Do that, then call for help if you see anything. There is power in numbers—especially our numbers." He grew thoughtful. "Val, can you research the demon in your system? His last name is Diamond or Dexter, I think. Maybe his history will give us some insight into him. His strengths, weaknesses."

"Thanks for letting us know," Luna said. "Maybe Mom and I can put our heads together with the other witches to come up with a spell to send him back to hell."

Her mother, Nora, chuckled. "Good idea."

"In the meantime, we can come up with something to protect Lyndsey," Twyla said.

Solis, Luna, and Twyla gathered around Nora as she approached David. "Yes. We'll need a picture and information about Caleb while he was human. If you can get that, then send it to us. We'll use his birthdate, birthplace, and astrological sign to develop a protection potion for Lyndsey."

"Great. I'll send you the information. Or Val may beat me to it. Whoever digs it up first," David said, sending a nod to Val, then eyeing his friends. "Thanks. Anything that will help is appreciated."

"Thank you," Lyndsey said. "It's so kind of you to help a total stranger."

"We're all on the same path," Twyla responded. "We must help one another."

Lyndsey nodded, appreciating their kindness. Yet, at the same time, she was apprehensive. She didn't know if she wanted to rely on some witches' potion for protection. Her gaze shot to David. Now, *he* seemed far more reliable.

David roamed the halls of the mansion, checking the doors were locked. He had a thing about the angels and other residents coming and going into the house after he went to bed, but he worked to control his anxiety over it.

Judging from the silence in their rooms, Lyndsey and Justin both seemed to be sleeping as far as David could tell.

In his room, he sat at his desk and fired up his computer to search for information about Caleb. It wouldn't be as easy as one might think.

He began with St. Paul, and he would expand his search radius from there. That was where Caleb had mowed him down, after all. Perhaps he'd lived there at the time.

David took a stab at his age. In his demon form, he'd still look the age he had been when he'd died, just as David did. So he added, *born in 1965-1975* to his search, guessing Caleb was somewhere between thirty-five and forty-five. Then he added, *deaths* and the name *Caleb*. He fed the criteria into the search engine.

A few Calebs with photos came up. None was his guy.

Then it occurred to David that Caleb, given his personality, might have a criminal record. He added that to the search criteria, expanded the age range by two years on both ends, and widened the location to include all of Minnesota, Wisconsin, and the Chicago area.

He sat back as he waited for the list to materialize. It popped up. It was amazing how quickly computers sorted through data.

He scrolled over a list of names with pictures. On the sixth page, he found his demon: Caleb Dexter of Savage, MN.

Found you.

David printed every bit of information he could find. He'd let the witches decide what was pertinent. Then he captured a snapshot of the data with his cell phone and messaged it to them, as well as to Val. It wouldn't hurt for the sheriff to know who they were dealing with. Besides, a potion would be a good backup plan, but not something he could rely on.

Caleb Dexter, born at 3:33 AM on December 12, 1974, in Savage, MN. Both parents killed in a house fire. He and the dog survived. He was raised in an orphanage until the age of fifteen when he fled—wanted for murder.

At nine the following morning, Grady ushered Nora into the kitchen. David, Justin, and Lyndsey had finished breakfast, and they were now discussing the day's schedule. Sissy LaFleur and Vincent, two of the angels who lived at the mansion, strolled through, selecting some sweet rolls.

"We're heading for a game of basketball. Anyone want to join us?" Vincent asked.

Justin jumped up. "I'm in. Lead the way."

They passed in front of Grady and Nora with a wave.

"I didn't expect you so soon," David said to Nora.

"He wasn't that complicated," she said. "Here you go." She handed a bottle to Lyndsey. "Take six drops, placed beneath the tongue, every three to six hours."

"What will this do, exactly?" Lyndsey asked, examining the bottle of blue fluid. She gave it a shake. It seemed thick, more like the consistency of honey than water.

"Turn you into a frog," Nora joked, then laughed until her eyes teared. She wiped a finger beneath her lids. "Sorry. It could be lack of sleep." Then she sobered. "The potion will make you undetectable to Caleb. He wouldn't be able to find you even if you were standing right in front of him. But," she cautioned, "don't drop it. If the glass container breaks, it will change the composition and could react in an unstable way."

"Thank you for getting this to us so quickly." Rising, he stood and hugged Nora. "You're the best."

Lyndsey held the bottle up to the light. "What's in it?"

"Mainly herbs from Twyla's garden. A witch never shares her potions," Nora said.

"Frogs and snails and puppy dogs tails," Lyndsey recited the nursery rhyme.

"Just don't skip a day," Nora warned. "And let me know when you're getting close to running out, and I'll make more."

"Okay. Thank you so much," Lyndsey said. "I appreciate your help."

"You're welcome, dear. We supernaturals need to stick together against the evil in the world." Nora clasped Lyndsey's hand in both of hers.

Lyndsey avoided correcting her, not saying she didn't consider herself one.

With a wave from Nora, David walked her to the front door.

While they were gone, Lyndsey opened the bottle. Immediately, she was assailed with a strong odor of garlic and something fishy. She involuntarily gagged. Oh my goodness, she didn't know if she'd be able to get it down. But she should begin with the drops right away.

She was trying to prepare herself for the taste when David walked back in. "That bad, huh?"

"Smell it." She held it out. When he took a whiff, he coughed.

"You'll need a chaser." He went to the refrigerator. "Coke or ginger ale?"

"Coke." It had a stronger taste, but it was about to be ruined. She held up the dropper. "Get it ready," she instructed, indicating the soda.

He popped the top and held it out. Holding her breath, as well as her nose, she counted out six drops under her tongue, closed her eyes, forced it down her throat, and snatched the Coke from his hand. It took a second for her to realize the potion didn't taste bad at all; it reminded her of cherries. She breathed a sigh of relief. "It only smells bad. The taste is okay."

"Good. I'm glad."

She stepped forward, planted a kiss on his mouth, and turned away. "I'm going to put this in my room."

With far more energy in her step than what should have been there considering a demon was after her, she danced into her bathroom and set the bottle on the counter beside the sink. She paused, looking in the mirror. Had she taken a magical potion made by a witch? What had she been thinking? Was there a blue sheen to her eyes? She leaned in closer to the mirror to examine the whites of her eyes. Nora had joked about turning her into a frog, but what effect *would* the potion have on her? All medications had some sort of side effects. Did potions?

When she went back out to the family room, David had a fire going. "Come sit for a while before we make a plan for the day."

"I'd like that," she said, following him to the sofa. She sat, getting comfortable. He handed her a mug of hot chocolate and joined her, wrapping an arm around her shoulders and pulling her close. She leaned against him, enjoying the feel of his muscular chest and arms around her. He felt strong and safe.

The heat of the fire warmed her, the crackling sound comforting and familiar, and his presence gave her peace. She fell asleep right there in his arms.

When she awoke, she was alone on the sofa. The fire had dimmed to a glow. She wasn't quite sure about the time. A faint memory surfaced—one of David, covering her with a throw. A warmth settled in her chest. She liked how considerate and caring he was beneath his hard exterior. He'd pulled the blanket over her, then whispered something she couldn't remember. But she did remember sighing in response.

The next thing she knew, midday sunlight shone through the double window. She curled onto her side, reluctant to rise.

From across the mansion, she heard the sound of dogs yipping and the clap of a door closing came. She wondered if David had taken the dogs outside.

She rolled to sit up, stretched, and padded to the kitchen. Immediately, the rich, dark aroma of coffee drifted to her. Evidently, during the winter months, Grady kept a pot on throughout the day. She paused at the counter where a perfect display of lunch fare had been set up. She poured herself a cup, added cream and sugar, then moved to the window, sipping the hot coffee and gazing out at David playing with his dogs. A fresh coat of snow had fallen. Tank ran, plowing through it and diving nose-first into the white powder. The two Pomeranians danced and barked with shrill, playful yips before the pair disappeared into a patch of snow. David laughed, leaned forward, and pulled them out. The pups wiggled in a licking frenzy, lapping at David's face. He gave a chest-rumbling laugh, the sort that made her feel good down to her toes. He truly had a special way with the animals, an ease. His caring and compassion showed in his gentle touch.

Without her permission, something stirred deep inside her. Lyndsey wanted to be around him more. She wanted to see how far this feeling would take her.

The door swung open then, and David and the dogs bounded in from the mudroom on the far side of the kitchen, shaking off the snow. "Hello, sleepyhead," he said, seeming happy and free of troubles. "Did you have a nice nap?"

"Yes, thank you. I'm not sure why I was so tired," she replied. "I like watching you with the dogs. You're good with them."

"*They* are good with *me*." He chuckled. "They make me feel human."

She nodded. It was easy to forget he was an angel. Part of her wished it weren't so.

"What are your plans for the day? I'd like to go into town for a while this afternoon. See it in the daylight. Go to the bookstore. You know, discover what inspires me. Would you like to join me?"

"Sure. I'd be glad to take you. Just give me a time."

She smiled. "How about we leave at one?"

"Sound's good. I have to meet with Val. I think I'm

going to ask Solis to meet up with us. She can hang with you. That way, you're not alone."

"I'm sure I'll be okay. But I like Solis. Either way is fine with me."

She headed upstairs to get dressed, then took her potion again—it wasn't as bad the second time around—and was back in the kitchen in time for Grady to deliver her a bottle of water before she'd even asked. She could get used to this.

David entered.

And she could get used to him. Her heart did a silly flutter as he strolled into the room in that confident way of his. "Ready?"

Oh yes. She was ready for a date—maybe more. But the thought came to a halt when she realized she didn't even know if angels could make love. She felt the heat rise to her cheeks as she hurried past him and out of the front door.

After getting her phone number so he could text her, he dropped her off in front of Fire and Fancy Books. Solis had agreed to meet Lyndsey, and they were going to hang out for a while. He watched Lyndsey hug Solis, enter the revolving door, and then disappear, tamping down the queasy sensation in his stomach. "You've taken the potion, right?"

"Yes. I'm good."

She'd wanted to find something to read to pass the time with on what she was now calling her "vacation." And for once, she didn't have her camera over her shoulder.

As soon as she was out of sight, he missed her. With a sigh, he scratched his head. What was happening to him? He'd lived in Terror for twenty-five years, watched it grow and become a landing place for supernatural creatures of all kinds. And never in all those years had he felt the urge to forget all that he held sacred to follow the unknown. He drove around the block, then headed for the sheriff's office to speak with Val.

Val lounged behind his desk, with his feet propped up and his keyboard across his thighs. He tapped the keys in rapid succession as he eyed the monitor.

"Find anything?" David asked as he walked over to the sheriff.

"Not much. Caleb died from a shotgun injury. His ex-wife claimed he tried to rape and beat her. She shot him in self-defense."

"Oh, Christ." David let out a long breath.

Frowning, Val met David's gaze. "I wouldn't be surprised if he carries around a special hatred for women in general."

Fire and Fancy Bookstore occupied the corner of Nevermore and S. 8th. It had been some other kind of store at one time. Lyndsey tilted back her head, taking in the stained-glass window of swirling vines and purple flowers that was positioned over the entrance. Matching display windows framed a revolving door. Solis pushed a section pane and entered. Lyndsey followed her, taking the next quarter slot.

The interior was a mix of clean and fresh with a bouquet of purple and pink flowers sitting on the small table to the right and refurbished old-world with white-washed brick walls, oak floors, and a wrought iron spiral staircase that led to a mezzanine.

"This is a beautiful store," she said to Solis.

"It is. I come here a lot."

"Hi, Solis," a woman standing behind the service

counter said. Her blonde hair draped over her shoulders in soft waves.

"Hey," Solis replied as they walked deeper into the store. "Lyndsey, this is the bookstore owner, Annabelle Thomas."

"Pleased to meet you," Lyndsey said.

"What can I help you with?" Annabelle asked.

"Where's your romance section?"

"They're over against the far wall. New books shelved at the top, used at the bottom."

Solis waved a hand. "I know where the mysteries are."

They headed in the same direction until Solis veered off an isle before the romance books. Lyndsey went for her favorite authors, listed alphabetically, selecting a mixture of historical romance, romantic suspense, and one paranormal…well, just because. She picked her six books, the number she usually bought at a one time, then headed to check-out. Traveling with her e-reader was so much more convenient. She wondered where it had ended up among her stored belongings.

Solis met her at the counter with her small stack of two books. "I guess you're kind of confined with having to stay away from a demon and all," she said, eyeing her load.

Annabelle said, "A girl after my own heart."

The woman didn't say anything about the demon comment. Maybe that kind of thing happened often in Terror. Lyndsey wasn't going to ask.

"I think I saw a coffee shop on the way here. Want to grab some?" Lyndsey asked.

"Sure. Caffeinated Corpse's Cappuccino is just down the street."

Swinging a cute little bag with the store's logo, a bonus for buying so many books, Lyndsey exited onto the sidewalk. After she texted David she was going for coffee, she crossed Nevermore Lane and walked down a block to the coffee shop. A raven seemed to follow them, flying from a rooftop to a telephone wire to the sign for the coffee shop. "The town seems to have a lot of birds," she said.

Solis chuckled. "I guess they're our town mascot."

Lyndsey shivered, quickly entering the café. "Reminds me of the Alfred Hitchcock movie, *The Birds*."

"Hmm. Haven't thought about that."

Lyndsey paused, glancing out the window as an older woman crossed the street. Her gray hair was a messy knot on top of her head. She wore a long coat, unbuttoned down the front, and shuffled along as if her knee or hip hurt her when she walked. Strange, she hadn't seen many older people at the bonfire the other night. Actually, she hadn't seen any elderly at all. Maybe it was too cold for them.

She reached for her camera, but realized she'd left it at the mansion. There was something unusual about the woman, and she would have liked to capture her photo. She touched her phone in her back pocket, taking it out.

"How ya doin'," the young man with wiry hair and a thin face behind the counter asked.

"Great, Burt," Solis answered. They both traveled to the counter, then made a selection.

Lyndsey ordered a coffee before finding an available table. She sat, the hot cup warming her cold hands, and took a sip. She was savoring the tasty liquid trickling down her throat when her phone pinged. She looked at her screen to find a message from David. It said he would meet her there in a few minutes.

Outside, the older woman hobbled across the street. Lyndsey snapped a few pictures on her phone. The woman fell and cried out. "My ankle," she moaned.

Lyndsey jumped from her seat, then rushed outside to the woman. "Are you all right?" she asked, taking hold of the woman's elbow and helping her to her feet while taking as much of the stranger's weight as she could. "Can you put pressure on it?"

Lyndsey felt the woman's weight shift, her entire body balancing on its own as if she hadn't even fallen. "Does it—" She glanced into the woman's face, which broke into a smirk that stopped Lyndsey cold. The woman cackled, morphing before Lyndsey's eyes. The silver hair grew darker, the wrinkled skin turning to bristly stubble.

This is a supernatural town, she reminded herself. *Maybe this is another creature I just don't know.*

Within a few seconds, the transformation was complete. "Caleb," she gasped. She knew it was the demon, could feel it in her bones.

He grabbed hold of her with both hands and dragged her through space and time, away from the coffee shop, away from people.

David entered the coffee shop, spotting Solis at the counter doctoring her latte. He did a three-sixty. Lyndsey was nowhere in sight. But there was a large stack of books on an empty table and a cup of coffee. He placed his hand on the container. It was still hot. "Where's Lyndsey," he asked Solis. She spun around, surprise written on her face as she looked between him and the table.

"She was just here," Solis said. "Maybe she went to the bathroom."

Panic hit him square in the chest, causing bile to rise in his throat. Dammit, the whole point of having Solis come along was to keep an eye on Lyndsey. He pressed his lips together as he jogged down a hallway to check the bathroom. When he knocked, all he heard was silence. He opened the door to find it empty.

"Lyndsey!" he hollered.

Only his voice echoed back at him in the hall. She wasn't there. He spun on his heel, then sprinted back out front.

"Are those her books?" he asked Solis when he returned.

"Yes. She was just here. I don't understand. I was putting cinnamon in my drink, trying to remember a movie she'd mentioned. It's an oldie. I hadn't seen it…"

"What movie?" Would that be a clue?

"*The Birds*."

He scrunched his brow. She was right—it was an old film.

He stepped toward the counter, asking the barista if she'd seen a pretty woman with brown hair who owned the books left on the table. "She went to help an elderly woman outside. I didn't see where they went."

Fear gripped David. As sure as he knew the sky was blue, he knew she had been snatched by the demon. He felt it in the marrow of his bones. He wanted to blame Solis for letting her guard down. But the truth was it was his fault for leaving her.

How could he have trusted her with someone else? He slammed one fist into the palm of his other hand so hard one of the small bones cracked loudly, snapping. But he could barely feel it. The only person he'd cared about in twenty-five years, and he'd left her in harm's way. David dropped into the nearest chair. He could smell her scent, see her brilliant smile, feel her hand resting over his. And now she could be suffering horribly.

He ran his hand through his hair, tugging the strands hard. "How did he find her?"

"Why didn't the potion work?" Solis voiced his next thought.

"Yeah, why?" He shot Solis a penetrating gaze.

"I…I don't know. Something in our information must have been wrong. His birthdate, birth location, parents… take your pick. The spell is only as good as the info. Garbage in, garbage out."

They hadn't given him the statistics. Or mentioned the possibility of messing up.

But he couldn't just sit there and lament the situation. He had to do something. He bolted out the door, threw back his head, and growled at the sky, at the unfairness of it. He set his hand on the hilt of his sword, double-checking he was armed, and spread his wings. But where should he look?

The McGuires.

Perhaps the witches would know… God, he hoped they would. "I'm going to speak to your mother," he bit out.

"What do you want me to do? How can I help?"

You could have kept a closer eye on her, he wanted to scream. "Get her books. Check with the witches. Whatever you can think of." He launched into the air. He had to find her before it was too late.

He veered sharply to the east, flying faster and faster toward Nora's.

12

He landed at a run, partially folding his wings as he raced up the porch. "Nora!" he shouted as he hammered on the front door.

The old wooden door opened, and Nora gaped at him. "What's wrong?"

"He has Lyndsay. I let my guard down, and the potion didn't work." His breath came in hard exhales and deep inhales. "Is there any way you can figure out where they went?"

"Come in," she said, hurriedly stepping aside.

"Don't you have a crystal ball or something? Or can't you read the leaves, or whatever? So that you can see them?"

"I don't understand why the potion failed." She was moving slowly—far too leisurely for the urgency of the situation. He wanted to shake her.

"It doesn't matter unless it's a clue to where he's taken her. I don't think it could have been far."

"He's delivering her to Lucifer for some reward." He clenched his hands.

"While *he* can travel wherever he wants, that's not the case with a human. He will have limitations with her."

"I hope you're right."

"As long as she's alive." Nora's eyes held a measure of sorrow in them as they locked on his. "There has to be a piece of information we're missing."

David pulled out his phone, then flipped to the message he'd sent the witches the other night:

Caleb Dexter, born at 3:33 AM on December 12, 1974, in Savage, MN. Both parents killed in a house fire. He and the dog survived. He was raised in an orphanage until the age of fifteen when he fled—wanted for murder.

"Or some piece of that information we have is wrong," she said. "That could be why the potion didn't work."

He searched the photos he'd taken of records. "This one has the time of birth as 3:36."

She whipped her head around, the silver-and-black of her hair falling forward. "That could do it. Also, AM or PM."

"I don't know."

"To find her, I need something that belongs to her. Preferably an item she values."

"I'll be right back." Turning, he dashed outside. He spread his wings, then took off for Thurston Mansion.

He landed on the drive, then burst into the foyer. Both Grady and Justin came running. "What's wrong?" Justin asked.

"The demon has Lyndsey." The sickening truth of David's words hit him hard. His stomach clenched in a knot. "Go get Val, then meet me at Nora's."

His mind began to spin with worst-case scenarios. No. He'd find her. She would be okay. He hadn't given his life to save her only to lose her now. He hurried to her room, searching around for her camera. There was probably nothing she valued more. He found it on the dresser, then snagged it. Mere seconds later, he was soaring through the sky toward Nora's once more.

*

Caleb tossed her over his shoulder as if she were a bag of dog food he'd just bought. He traveled swiftly along the street with supernatural speed. She tried to keep track of where they were going.

"Put me down. I can walk, you know," she said.

He didn't say a word but kept moving away from the bookstore, away from Solis and David, away from safety.

He remained on Never More Lane until he came to the cemetery on his left. The entrance was framed by stone pillars topped with gargoyles that supported a set of huge wrought-iron gates.

She squeezed her eyes shut, fighting the urge to tense. Please, oh please, not the cemetery. In a town like Terror, that was the last place she wanted to be. Not that she wanted to be in the clutches of a demon.

He turned right.

She sighed.

His shoulder dug into her abdomen. Wincing, she twisted her head, noting they were on 11th Street now. Not that far from 8th. Would David be able to find her? Did angels have a unique power to hunt demons? She hoped so. But she was drawing at anything to stay calm.

When they came to the clock tower, he turned and climbed the front steps to the door. He set her feet on the cement terrace. She stumbled, but managed to catch her balance.

"Let me go."

He gave a haughty laugh. "You're mine now."

"No. David will find you. He'll…he'll…destroy you."

She didn't know exactly what David would do or how he'd do it. Kill him? Send him back to Satan? A tremor ran up her spine.

"Come on." He wrapped his long fingers around her wrist, then tugged her through the door into the clock tower. She tried to resist, grabbing hold of the doorframe and almost sitting on the ground, but he yanked her forward with little effort. She groaned as she staggered after him.

Inside, there were winding stairs and an elevator. She tipped her head, peering up. How many stories? Five? Seven?

He hauled her after him again, taking the staircase.

"The elevator would be quicker," she pointed out.

He shot her an evil stare. "It's not for me."

How wasn't it for him? She wanted to know…yet didn't care. Did he not like mechanical things? Did he have claustrophobia? Her wrist ached. He moved a lot quicker and easier than she did. She tripped, banging her knee on the step in front of her. He drew her along. "Slow down, will ya?"

By the fifth floor, she was winded. Her lungs and shoulder ached. "You can let me go on my own. Where will I run off to?"

He kept going. She gritted her teeth. Each floor was separated by a landing, where they would turn, and she'd get a small—*tiny*—break. She breathed hard. They passed the set of five bells, which would be a killer when they rang.

One more floor.

Finally, they reached the floor that housed the clock, and he let go of her. Stumbling, she held onto the railing to steady herself until she could breathe. Then she straightened, hitting him with her best death stare. "Really. Next time, take the elevator."

The view in front of her was spectacular. The sun perched high in the sky so it shone on the opaque face of the clock, emphasizing the clock face and casting shadows throughout the room. Giant mechanical gears turned ever so slowly.

Lyndsey slumped in the corner of the clock tower. Caleb droned on and on about the awful boredom he'd endured in the tiers of Purgatory, at how she needed to suffer the way he had, and how he shouldn't be too quick in killing her and taking her to Lucifer. He clearly liked to hear himself talk. She released a huge sigh, her breathing slowing as she tried to decide what to do next. At least she knew where she was. That was something.

She squinted, peering at him. Why hadn't the potion worked? It didn't matter now. She was five stories above the ground, and she would have to make it past a demon to get free.

She could hear the ravens squawking outside. There must have been hundreds. Suddenly, she wished she could fly. The thought made her smile. She'd fly right out the window, shocking Caleb.

But, of course, she couldn't fly. She concentrated on David, willing him to find her.

David presented the camera to Nora.

She nodded. "Yes, this will do. It's filled with her life-force." She opened a large, squat jar, dipped her index finger into it, and brought out a drop of tan-colored ointment. She carefully dotted the cream on several places on the camera. "This will act as a divining rod," she explained. "But don't worry. I won't put it anywhere that might ruin it. With this salve upon it, though, it will find its owner and lead you right to her. But you need to act quickly before the salve dissipates."

He took the camera from her. "Thank you," he said, then cupped his hand behind her head and drew her forward to place a big kiss on her forehead. He gave a shaky grin. "It's good luck to kiss a witch, isn't it?"

"I've never heard of that, but it sounds good to me," Nora said with a happy grin.

He spun around and headed out the door, allowing the camera to lead him. It was as if he were clinging to a magnet as it was drawn to iron.

The morning sun shone on his wings, warming them. He looked down at his shadow as he soared over the buildings. The camera was leading him east. He tried to figure out where it was taking him, recalling the bonfire celebration and the pictures Lyndsey had taken of him and Caleb. Suddenly, he had a feeling he knew where she was—the very place in those photos.

The camera pulled him forward, and, sure enough, the sensation grew stronger as they approached the clock tower. David landed on the balcony that encircled the tower, coming to a halt between the balustrade and the outer wall. He paused and listened. A glass double door was positioned below the clock for easy access to the mechanics both inside and out. He stood outside it, then leaned forward enough to view inside. Caleb peered into the clock face on the opposite wall.

David tried the door handle. It was unlocked. He guessed there wasn't a point to restricting people when they were five stories high.

Easing inside, he set her camera on the stone ledge by the door. He drew his sword, unsheathing the tempered steel as it expanded in length until it was longer than his outstretched arm. There were carvings on the hilt and halfway down the blade, the story of his right to protect good from evil. He took a deep breath. Lyndsey sat on the floor, her head resting forward on her knees. She had to be okay. Caleb better not have hurt her.

She glanced up, meeting his gaze. He brought his index finger to his lips, signaling silence.

13

David burst into the room, wielding his sword. His gaze darted around the dim, shadowed interior; the gray stone walls absorbed what light there was. He spotted Lyndsey huddled in the corner. She moved, her gaze lifting to his, her eyes appearing tired with blueish circles beneath them. Relief shot through him, so intense it bordered on painful. She was all right.

Shock spread over Caleb's face. He shot forward, placing himself in front of Lyndsey. A lime-green mist swirled from his hands, filling the space, making it hard to see and smell. "No. She's mine."

David raised the sword and brought it down in an arch, aiming for the spot where the demon's throat should have been. Instead, he sliced through the air. Flashes of black broke through the haze as Caleb flipped head-over-heels with a smooth aerial move, landing safely, yet farther away from Lyndsey.

He took the opportunity to maneuver his body

between them—anything to make it harder for Caleb to get his hands on her was good.

But Lyndsey didn't stay put. She crouched and traveled to the window where he'd entered. *What was she doing?* Maybe she would exit. That would be great. "Get out of here," he told her. He didn't want to take his eyes off Caleb, but he wanted to keep track of her.

She snatched her camera from the ledge, then whirled around and took aim at Caleb. Flashes of light came from the camera, lighting the inside of the tower. The mist illuminated with strobed blasts of light as if at a music concert.

Caleb's form seemed to change and shift into a horrible monster with a vulture-like head and long spindly arms. It jumped toward Lyndsey. Caleb swung his sword, striking the beast.

Instantly, the demon turned into black ash and fell to the ground, ash strewn on the cement floor, with several particles bursting into flame and burning out. The mist immediately began to dissipate and clear.

"Oh my God." Lyndsey's hands trembled on the camera. "You…you killed him."

He commanded the sword back to its normal size, then thrust it back in its sheath on his hip. "He was already dead. I just put him out of his misery." He reached down and stilled her hands, then pulled her up and drew her to him. "Are you all right? Did he hurt you?" He took a step back again to look at her.

She shook her head. "I'm… I'm fine. Simply scared."

"That was cool what you did with the camera. It was like it had an energy force of its own."

She shrugged. "Sometimes, my connection with the camera amazes me."

He wrapped an arm around her back, guiding her out the door into the sunlight.

"How did you find me?" she asked.

He'd imagined rescuing Lyndsey, of her being always his—forever found. Now they had a chance.

He peered at her camera she'd slung over her shoulder, and she followed his gaze. "My camera? Thank you for bringing it."

"Nora put a spell on it—a special honing salve so it would lead me to you."

"At least *that* spell worked." She rested her hand over her camera, feeling a strong pull. "I hope it's not ruined."

"It will wear off," he explained with a soft chuckle as they took the elevator to the ground floor. "Unlike me. You won't get rid of me so easily."

Standing outside the clock tower, she threaded her fingers in his hair and drew his head down, kissing him. She pulled back, gazing into his eyes. "Who said I wanted to?"

Justin and Val came running up the sidewalk. "You're okay," Justin said, sounding amazed and relieved.

She smiled at her cousin. "I'm fine. Maybe even better than fine."

"And Caleb?" Val asked, his gaze on the angel.

"Dead as dead can be," David said.

14

"Are you ready for this?" Lyndsey asked, wheeling a large suitcase by her side. It held most of her clothes—her favorite pieces anyway. The rest were in boxes in the back of his truck, along with her photography supplies. Thurston Mansion was about to get a new resident.

David leaned toward her to kiss her. "How messy can one photographer be?"

She knew he had the answer to that. He'd seen a photo of her St. Paul apartment, and he'd almost had a heart attack. She was a stacker. But she could always find whatever paper, picture, or article she needed on the first try. It was a far cry from anything close to the perfection he was used to at the mansion.

"Remember, you promised me my own office and *no meddling*."

He laughed. "You have my word. I'm nothing if not adaptable."

"So you keep saying." She quirked a brow.

Grady came into the hall, then took her suitcase. "Welcome home," he said.

She tilted her head up to gaze at David. His hair swept across one of his cheeks. Brushing it aside, he gently touched his scar. He still hadn't told her how he'd gotten it. She wondered if it had something to do with the truck that had killed him when he'd saved her and her mother.

"Have I told you I love you today?" he asked.

"Not in the last hour," she said with a laugh.

He kissed her then, long and slow. There was so much about him that was still a mystery. But that was okay. She had a lifetime to learn about him, and then an eternity in the afterlife.

She raised her camera, then snapped a picture of him going into their bedroom. One of the first things she wanted to figure out was how to capture his image in focus. Then she remembered. "Hey angel, show me your wings."

He shot her a wickedly playful grin as he slowly brought them out with a skillful flutter. She snapped the photo. Gotcha.

THE END

Thank you for reading *Forever Found*. If you enjoyed this story and want to stay up-to-date on my next book and release dates then sign up for my newsletter. (I promise your email address will never be shared and you can unsubscribe at any time.)

https://larissaemerald.com/contact/

Did you know that one of most awesome things you can do for an author is post a review? It doesn't need to be long, just a few lines will do, but a review goes a long way to help authors achieve visibility. So, if you enjoyed the book, share the news with a friend and take a few minutes to leave a review!

Read on for a sneak peek of **Perfection**.

Excerpt from

PERFECTION

CODE PERFECT SERIES

LARISSA EMERALD

CHAPTER 1

May 1, 2226

In a proficient dance of gears and balance, the robotic waitress slid breakfast onto the table before rolling away from the booth. Eggs, spinach, buffalo sausage, and coffee—his usual. Lieutenant York Richmond wrapped his fingers around the steaming cup of cloned Colombian, forgoing the undersized handle, and drew it to his lips. The steam, along with the familiar aroma, awakened his sinuses. Now if only it would nudge his brain and muscles to life.

"Rough night, huh?" Across from him, Detective Vivian Lester lined up her silverware on the table, then picked up the spoon and stirred cream into her coffee.

He shrugged at his partner's understatement. "Need to change families for a month or so, s'all."

"Guess it's kind of weird to arrest your mom."

"Well, you know Mom. Queen of protests." His mother fought for equality between Genetically Engineered Individuals and Coders, the descendants of the original human gene pool. She hated the direction of designer babies and the Committee's regulations that governed GEI and everyone else.

"Hey, there's an antiquities sale tomorrow. Want to go?"

He set aside the coffee, hit his eggs with equal shots of

Tabasco and mustard, and dug in. If Vi felt compelled to divert his attention to his hobby, then he must be a seriously sorry sight. His mouth edged into a reluctant smile, despite how tired he felt. "I'm good."

"Really?"

"Besides, I didn't arrest her. Technically, anyway. I just ensured she wasn't newsworthy by calming her down." The national media weren't after the truth—they were after a story. He stabbed his fork into a hunk of sausage, slid the utensil between his teeth, left the meat behind, and removed the metal. Peering at her across the table, he quirked a single brow.

With a contrite nod, she turned her attention to her French toast.

Vi treating him like a keepsake Christmas ornament was over. Really, she wanted to go hunting for antiques with him? Ever since Danny—

No. He put the brakes on that thought. Tapping his spot computer, he rested it in his palm as he searched the Chicago headlines for any sign of Amanda Richmond. *Nothing.*

Good for you, Mom.

The headlines focused on the World Health Organizations US regional convention, which was where his mother had been protesting. The broadcast showed dignitaries exchanging greetings. GEI and Coders filled the expansive hall at the Rhodium Hotel. To the casual eye, they seemed similar with their homogenized honey-brown skin from the mixed races blending over the years. But that was where the resemblances ended. Unlike throughout history, today's issue wasn't about race—it was about privilege. His mom was outspoken about equal genetic opportunities and restricting the push for more advancement.

He checked a few more sites for any different news, then paused. On the screen, a newscaster announced the discovery of yet another suicide by genetic mutation.

Instances of people shooting up with a genetic-alteration serum had reached epidemic proportions. The serum caused their genes to go haywire and mutate until they died, horribly. A shiver raced through him. He was glad he hadn't caught that case. It hit too close to home.

"So you want to go chumming around with me tomorrow, eh?" he asked.

Vi rolled her eyes.

He half chuckled. "I thought so. We could even make it a family affair—hook up with Mom, cousin Stacey, and the kids. Maybe even Cal."

"Let's leave your brother out of it. It's not Christmas or anyone's birthday, so I'm good." She stared at her breakfast as if engrossed. That was the problem with friends dating family. When the relationship didn't work out, things got awkward. Cal wanted Vi to quit the force. Vi didn't want to. End of relationship.

An announcement from the International Security Intelligence Generator of Human Tracking overrode York's info search, shocking the amused grin right off his face. The forkful of Tabasco-laced eggs he'd been eager to consume a millisecond earlier didn't make it into his mouth. He lowered his arm, the fork clanking against plastic. The sausage in his mouth turned bland and grainy, much like eating sand. The food scraped his throat as he swallowed. "What the hell?"

"What? Not your mom?"

"No. A message from InSIGHT." In disbelief, he read the accompanying post aloud, his appetite shriveling with every syllable. "Isabelle D-Gastion is dead."

Vi gasped. "That's impossible. She's GEI."

"Right, and genetically engineered individuals don't die without help, what with their perfect genes and all." York thumbed the valet button synced to his air-car's autopilot. "I've signaled for the car. Ready?" He scooted to the end of the booth, then stood.

"Guess so. Where are we going?"

"Fredrick B-Gastion's." His tone grim, he said, "If I've learned anything in the last few years, it's there's a first time for everything. And given she's the daughter of the World Health Organization's regional director, well, this can't be an accident."

Poor, innocent Isabelle. She was only two. He drew a deep breath. It felt like a heavy hand pressed over his heart.

As they exited the diner, a vocal emergency statement came through his comm, instructing them to report to the scene. Good thing, considering he was heading there anyway. Fredrick was a friend.

Daylight had broken, but, from where they stood, skyscrapers hid the sun. This early in the morning, the city still slept. In an hour or so, the streets and walkways would be bustling with people. For an instant, he was aware of the changing of the guard, so to speak. The hum of huge air purification filters on the nearby corner ceased. Chicago sat silent, expectant. He breathed in a whiff of smog-free air. This quiet moment rang false. Every part of him knew it.

His air-car pulled up to the curb, and they got in. After adjusting the thrusters for vertical ascent, he launched. Memos flashed over a nucleus screen set in the console, and his onboard computer kept up a running monologue of information and updates as he drove. The female voice sounded cool and collected. By the time he'd piloted from midtown to the swanky Chicago suburb on the lake, three notices indicated other units had arrived at the Gastion residence

He gripped the steering wheel. Had the child died of natural causes—which seemed impossible unless there'd been some sort of accident—or was someone targeting her father and the kid had gotten in the way? The WHO's regional director held jurisdiction over the Committee and its genetic selections, oversaw universal health emergencies, monitored the impact of climate and environmental change, and advocated for the Coder population. Dealing with those issues placed Fredrick B-Gastion in direct conflict with a lot of people. Was someone upset about a decision WHO had made? Were they angry enough to retaliate?

"Hand it over, ladybug," Kindra B-Zaika said with a gentle tone meant to coax her child into minding.

"No." Brianna stomped her foot, defiantly throwing her head back.

Stunned by her daughter's uncharacteristic explosive outburst, Kindra inhaled a calming breath.

"I want it to open *noooow*," Brianna wailed, drawing the final word into a quivering, nerve-scraping bleat.

Kindra touched cool fingers to her brow, then glanced out the panel of windows in the living room to discover dawn tiptoeing over the city. A streak of air traffic blazed in the distance, weaving between skyscrapers. People were on the move. But here she was, stonewalled by a two-year-old. She couldn't leave for work with Brianna so upset.

Her daughter held out the potted sunflower in her small hands. Her eyes glistened as her blue irises disappeared into rich-brown outer rims—a telltale sign of how distraught she was.

"The flower has a growth cycle. It's not time for it to bloom," Kindra explained.

Brianna thrust out her lower lip, then pitched the uncooperative plant to the floor. Kindra sighed, struggling for composure as she watched the melodrama of flailing arms and legs that followed. She'd never encountered such a tantrum, so she wasn't sure how to deal with it. What was happening to her sweet little girl? Such out-of-control behavior was a first. In fact, they'd bred D-Generation to have an even temperament.

Worried, Kindra folded her hands, then touched a

knuckle to her lips. She was reluctant to play the waiting game, but what else could she do? She tried to think of solutions, from sending Brianna to timeout to making her clean up the mess to scolding her. But she was only two. Would those punishments even work?

It'll pass.

Kindra had a gazillion items on her overloaded agenda. Just the thought of presenting her controversial report to the Genetics Committee right when she arrived at the office made her shudder. Nausea roiled in her stomach. The Committee had gotten power hungry lately, and they didn't care to have their authority challenged. She needed quiet. She needed solitude. She needed to rehearse her pitch.

"Fifteen minutes," Nanny Sally advised as she entered the room.

"Yes, I know," Kindra said when the popular-model android began to tick off five-minute increments in an effort to get her to work on time. *Fooltar.* She could do without the nanny's annoying programming this morning.

Near the electric-blue sofa, she knelt beside her daughter. A thrashing foot clipped Kindra's shin, snagging her leggings. She winced, then stroked Brianna's forehead. *Be calm, please.*

Brianna stilled at her mother's touch, turning big, watery eyes up.

"Ladybug, you can't *make* the flower bloom just because you want it to."

With several hiccups, Brianna tried to control her crying.

Kindra collected the pot, replaced a handful of spilled soil, and set it upright on the floor. She settled cross-legged next to the plant, then spied the gel book on the end table. Perhaps a pretend flower would do in the interim. She extended her hand, concentrated, and summoned Brianna's holographic computer with a flare of psychokinesis.

Stilling, Brianna peered at her. She sniffed back tears with sudden interest.

Kindra smothered a thankful sigh. Distraction. Perfect. She skipped her fingers over the gel book, bringing the electronic images to life until she accessed the file she wanted. "What color would you like your flower to be?"

"Yellow. Intense yellow."

Intense, of course—Brianna's word of the week. Last week, it was *activate*. A rush of pride swelled inside Kindra at her daughter's advanced intelligence. All children of D-Generation were geniuses, as mandated by the Committee. They would be attend university by age nine.

Kindra sighed. *Such potential.*

These kids were far beyond what she had been as a child, more intelligent, more intuitive, and more talented. Even though Kindra graduated high school at thirteen, university at seventeen, and worked alongside her father learning the ins and outs of genetics, she wondered if she had even a hope of keeping up when the Ds grew into adults.

With another swirl of her finger, a vibrant sunflower popped up from the page. Kindra carefully detached the 3D creation, separating it from the book. "This will have to do until I get home this evening."

"But it's May Day. I wanted to give you a *real* flower."

Downy, soul-deep warmth caressed Kindra's insides. "I appreciate that. But some things can't be rushed." She smiled. The urge to stay home from work tempted her. "Come here." She patted her leg, inviting Brianna to sit on her lap.

Her little girl scooted over, sniffled again, then snuggled closer, surveying the wounded plant. Kindra caressed her sweet oval face, smoothing silky strands of blond hair away from eyes that were gradually returning to their lively crystal blue. Like mother, like daughter. Brianna was sensitive, intuitive, and demanding. Kindra smiled, amazed at how a genetically engineered D-Generation— one far superior to her own B-Generation—were created with such scientific precision, yet remained so defined by age emotionally.

"I'll bring a freshly blooming flower home with me when I return from work, okay? This one"—she firmly tamped down the soil around the base of the stem—"will take a few days to open."

Brightening, Brianna tilted her head with an impish nod. "Not a cloned one."

Where do kids learn these things?

"I'll do my best." Kindra wrapped her arms around Brianna, breathing in her little-girl scent. When had this child she'd rescued from the embryo-discard bin come to mean so much to her? It had been an impulsive, weak moment. The Committee had discarded so many embryos. Kindra had felt if she could save at least one, it would fill the void inside her. But as time passed and she learned more about being a mother, the more her discontent with the Committee grew.

Brianna filled Kindra's heart with love, leaving it aching in its intensity. Had her own mother ever cared for her this way?

Doesn't matter.

She shook her head when Brianna wiggled out of her arms. Clearly ready to play, her child swept up a doll from a nearby chair.

Kindra stood. "How about if you and Chloe do a unity session? The quiet time will help you center yourself."

Brianna headed down the hall without a backward glance. "Can't," she said before disappearing through her bedroom door, Chloe hugged to her chest.

Kindra's breath snagged in her throat, and she frowned. Brianna had never refused the spiritual exercise. Another warning signal tripped—an additional odd occurrence. First the tantrum. Now this.

With her usual rigid posture and head tilt that didn't displace a single dark hair, Sally held out a square box housing Kindra's computer key, the coded chip she needed to access files at work. "Time to go."

Fingers curling around it, Kindra ripped her attention from her daughter. "Call me if she gets upset again."

"I will. Don't forget my updated replacement arrives tomorrow."

"Yes. I have it in my system," Kindra said absently, grabbing her satchel from the foyer table. As she closed the door behind her, she couldn't shake the mother's intuition telling her something bigger was wrong with Brianna.

She shook her head. Perhaps it was simply growing pains. Brianna had a birthday soon.

He jogged up to Gina just as she was unlocking the apartment door. She jumped. He took hold of her hands, pulling her abruptly toward him. As he was a little winded and a lot exited, a moment passed before he could speak. "It's done."

"What are you talking about?" Blankly, she stared, leaning backward so her sunflower-blonde hair draped down her back. Her fine, sculptured brows knit with confusion.

He wanted to grab a fistful of hair and tug her into submission, but he resisted. He was a man of willpower, after all. Didn't his planning and careful execution of his idea prove that?

"Remember when I mentioned I'd discovered a way to make them pay for their slights over the years? To once and for all show them I was just as smart and capable as their top scientists?" *God, he longed to share his accomplishment. She'd be so proud of him.*

"What did you do?" she asked hesitantly.

Smoothing his fingers over her cheek, he changed his mind about telling her. He didn't want anything to dampen his mood, his elation. "Nothing. Never mind. We'll talk about it tomorrow." He interlocked his fingers with hers, then led her into the apartment and his bedroom.

CHAPTER 2

York parked alongside B-Gastion's Air-Porsche on the second floor of the landing garage, as he had for past visits. He admired the Porsche while he and Vi strolled between the vehicles. B-Gastion had chosen a fancy family flyer while York had gone for sleek power.

"You're going to get in trouble for parking here," Vi complained.

"Maybe. But I don't think the captain's speech about not ruffling the locals' feathers referred to active investigations."

They didn't speak as they navigated the stairs to a private access. A wall of shrubbery kept them hidden until they were almost to the front door. A crowd had gathered halfway up the walkway, which was framed by low, manicured hedges. Vehicles filled the street. "Damn. Every reporter in town must have intercepted the police stream."

"Better here than at your mom's arrest. Benefited her situation, don't you think?"

"Nah, too much time had lapsed. Just a lucky break." But this morning *had* been too easy. Coincidence? The media types trolled for headlines, and they had the money to support their efforts. Of course, GEIs were far too interested in what was happening in their own circles to invest much effort in the imperfect world of Coders. But...

Screw it. York had other worries right now.

His spot computer thrummed against his hand. He checked it while he walked. The data readout darkened, adjusting to the sunlight piercing the clouds in the east. InSIGHT had updated the status of Isabelle's investigation with photos and preliminary stats of body temperature and decomposition. York studied the images of tiny Isabelle lying on the floor of a child's bedroom, a doll clutched to her chest. A knot lodged in his throat. He shivered, and his stomach clenched. York wouldn't wish this tragedy on the genetic misfits hiding in the tunnels, let alone on a valued friend.

As regional director, B-Gastion had built strong partnerships with other nations committed to accelerating progress toward global development goals of health surveillance and reducing health inequalities. In the eighty years or so since the GEIs had stepped into the vast majority of power jobs in society, the position had been held by a GEI, and his policy usually favored the wealthy. Even so, when York's boy was ill, B-Gastion was the only GEI who attempted to help him.

York inhaled a breath, held it, then moved on with the exhale. He could feel Vi watching him, probably wondering how he was holding up. *Solid,* he wanted to tell her, but he didn't.

Beneath the stately columned portico, Fredrick B-Gastion greeted them with the formality one would expect from a dignitary. His spine held him erect, but the forward dip of his shoulders and grief in his eyes gave him away. "Thank you for coming so promptly, Lieutenant."

"Of course." York clasped his friend's extended hand. "I'm not sure if you've met my partner, Detective Vivian Lester."

"I have, but I can't remember where at the moment."

Vi angled her head. "I wish this meeting were under different circumstances, sir."

Didn't they all?

No matter appearances, B-Gastion had to feel hurt and broken. The evidence rang clear in the regional director's half-hearted handshake and emotion-reddened eyes.

"Let's go inside." York urged B-Gastion toward the half-open door.

Vi trailed them. Their feet rapped an uneven rhythm on the glossy marble tiles as they moved deeper into the house. He and B-Gastion stopped when they reached the living area. They stared at each other, professional to professional, man to man, father to father.

"Who made the discovery?" York asked. The anguish on B-Gastion's face said he may have reached his threshold for holding it together. York placed an arm around his friend's shoulder, then directed him toward the sofa. B-Gastion pulled away without taking a seat.

"Her mother." B-Gastion's voice broke on the last word, and he cleared his throat. "How…how could this happen? It's not supposed to happen."

York smothered a curse. "We'll find out. I'm so sorry."

"This is… It's such a shock." Fredrick pressed his lips together, then averted his eyes.

"The sooner we start the investigation, the quicker we'll have answers," Vi said gently. "Where's Isabelle's room?"

Fredrick glanced at the staircase. His face crumpled, mouth quivering.

York stood tall, wishing he could loan his friend his strength. "We can find our way. Why don't you sit for a few?"

Drawing a breath, B-Gastion appeared to suck back his emotion as best he could. "No. No, I should go with you."

"It's all right. The ME and the forensic team will arrive soon. You can usher them in." York sought words of comfort, but he knew it was impossible. Condolences wouldn't grant B-Gastion what he wanted most. So York slipped a recorder ring from his finger and held it out, a stall technique to give the other man time to compose himself. "Dictate every detail you can remember. The daily routine. If anyone new has been in the house. Anything and everything."

B-Gastion took the ring, then eased it over his thumb with shaky fingers.

A few minutes later, York and Vi stood in the center of the dead two-year-old's room. Inconceivable. Sprawled on the floor, she looked so alone dressed in her pale pink pajamas covered in cartoons renditions of black-and-white kittens. Tightening his hold on his crime-scene kit, he struggled for perspective. If he could shut out the sound of weeping coming from the room next door—surely B-Gastion's wife—it would make his task a hell of a lot easier.

He knelt beside the Isabelle's D-Gastions small body. Blond hair framed a delicate face, brushing her shoulders. The child could have been in a deep sleep, hugging a lookalike Global Doll.

Exhaling a shuddering breath, he fought the sting in his eyes. It had been six years since he'd faced the death of someone this young, and his son's passing had not been so peaceful. His hand shook as he opened the crime-scene bag. Images of his boy flashed in his mind—a toothless grin, a small hand tossing a red ball, thin arms wrapped tightly around his neck.

Briefly, he squeezed his eyes shut before opening them.

The quiet sound of Vi's voice brought his head up. Standing on the opposite side of Isabelle, she dictated information into her spot computer.

She met his gaze. "Hey, I didn't consider it earlier, but why did the captain assign this one to us? It's not our RO."

"Rotation doesn't come into play here. B-Gastion requested me."

She angled her head. "Oh, right."

York sensed her watching him, perhaps searching for a

reaction. He just passed his med-scanner over the girl, watching the monitor for any sign of physical trauma but finding none.

"This doesn't make sense, Vi. No trauma. And GEIs don't die, even in accident situations. Primps can put them back together with cloning and such."

"Unless the injury is to the head. The brain is the one organ that can't be cloned."

The health packages for GEIs far exceeded the basic medical unit of immunity to disease and illness granted to Coders like York. The genetic code of Coders remained largely unaltered. When they did get alterations, they were the kind that attached to stem cells and altered the genes from the outside in, as opposed to the ground-up method from inception used with GEIs. In the early years of genetic engineering, participating in the new science had required money. *Perfection* had cost a hefty sum.

So did saving a life, he thought bitterly. *Even a young one.*

Vi averted her gaze from the girl's body. "Yeah, strange."

After he shoved the test equipment into his bag, he roughly zipped it. "There isn't a mark on her. Nothing."

"Then what killed her?" Vi's voice snagged.

York stood. "You okay?"

She nodded, but avoided eye contact. He knew better than to believe her. It was a code of denial they shared.

"Any guesses?"

Crossing his arms to control the tightness in his chest, he shrugged. "Some sort of asphyxiation, maybe? Poison? I don't know."

His QuL beeped in his ear, and he responded with a brusque, "York."

"When are you going to get rid of that QuickLink? It's a dinosaur," Vi whispered. Then she held up a hand, talking more to herself than to him. "I know, I know. Less likely to be traced by criminals."

He rolled his eyes, focusing on Captain Avery's voice.

As usual, the captain sounded worried. He was probably getting hit from all sides. Damn politics. Avery asked for a crisis update. York obliged with a list of stats. "We're treating this like a suspicious death until we learn differently. We'll check out any contacts. Wait to see if there are demands. Maybe it's extorsion gone bad."

York listened to his superior's instructions. Grimacing, he said, "Right. One of us will go over there."

He disconnected.

"Now what?" Vi asked.

"Avery wants one of us to fetch a geneticist since we don't have an expert on staff. Then take 'em to the morgue to evaluate the...*situation.*"

She pursed her lips, then shifted her attention to wrapping up her notes.

"Vi? Talk to me." At her obvious reluctance, he added their customary, "Flip you for it." He withdrew his lucky coin from his pocket. It was a 1976 quarter from the days when they actually used coins.

Slowly, she shook her head.

Finally, she curled her spot computer into her chest. Good thing it was made from flexible materials. It appeared as if she were going to crush it in her hand. Her almond-shaped eyes blazed. "You know how I hate those scientists."

"Like I don't?"

"Will you do it? Please?"

He glanced around the room, taking in the perfect environment of a model GEI child. Just two weeks ago, he'd bounced the sweet, laughing girl on his knee. Something horribly strange was going on. Damn it, for little Isabelle D-Gastion, he would set aside his personal feelings and unearth the truth. He'd work with those high-and-mighty scientists even if it killed him.

"Don't worry. This one's mine." No way he'd be satisfied with anyone else handling the case, anyway. A door clacked shut downstairs, then voices echoed throughout the house—probably the forensic team. "But you owe me a pizza," he added.

"Deal," she said without hesitation. Tucking her hair behind her ear, she forced out a heavy sigh. "Guess we should let go of this hatred eventually."

"Never."

"Did the captain ask for any geneticist in particular?"

York lifted the test bag. "Wouldn't you know—he wants that hardnosed B-Zaika." He didn't know her personally, but the lead scientist of the Seville Genetics Center was always on the news. York could envision her beautiful smile as she hawked her latest creation to the public in her slight English accent.

With an exaggerated consoling pat on the back, Vi said, "Sorry."

"Sure." York thought he heard a good-humored snicker behind him as they stepped out of the bedroom and into the hall. God knew they needed something to ease the sting of leaving that poor little girl behind.

A pair of sweepers arrived first. They would check all the electronics in the room. Next came the ME and a couple of uniforms. York acknowledged Shishido, the officer in charge of the forensics team, then addressed the group. "Test for foreign substances, poison. Check the toys, gel books, clothes, everything. Whatever killed her may be on anything she touched. Take their Nanny Sally back to our lab, too. I want an e-specialist to go over all security and electronics. And we're going to want to talk with anyone who has access to the house."

The others nodded. With a look, he passed the command to Vi, then went downstairs after she took the team into the bedroom. B-Gastion now sat on the sofa where York had left him. There were people moving around him—technicians going over every inch of the place and more uniforms documenting everything, all searching for evidence that would tell them what had killed a GEI child.

Fredrick started to rise, but York motioned for him to stay put. Better to remain out of the techs' way. "You done with that?" he asked, indicating the recorder ring.

Slowly, the dazed man nodded and handed it over.

York slipped it onto his finger. "I'll need to talk to Isabelle's mother, of course, and your staff. Also, I'll need a list of your enemies. People who aren't happy with your policies, whoever you can think of who might want to cause trouble or hurt you, etcetera." His voice softened. "And if you think of anything else, or if there's anything I can do, call me."

B-Gastion rubbed the back of his neck. "Thank you."

York gave a curt nod. "I'll be back later."

Vi waited for him at the gigantic double panel doors. As he walked closer, all the anger and frustration, pain and memories, twisted into a colossal knot in his chest. He'd forgotten rule number one—*don't allow people to get too close because it hurts like hell.*

He thought he'd learned that lesson. He'd thought he was numb.

God, he'd thought *wrong.* His dismay over investigating the death of a child weighed on him. With a white-knuckled grip on the brass handle, he glanced at his partner and threw open the door. "Get ready for the piranhas."

They'd gotten in behind the cover of the landscaping, but exiting would not be so easy.

Vi quickly stepped out, almost breaking into a run. York matched her pace. It was standard in such situations, but that didn't mean he had to like it. They hadn't made it far before reporters bombarded them. Within inches of bursting through the wall of news people lining the pristine lawn, York halted. "Get the hell out of my way."

No one budged. Fine. He'd enjoy mowing them down. It was *that* kind of day.

A cluster of tiny drone cameras—Tracers—hovered overhead. At times like this, York detested procedure. In his experience, rules weren't necessarily the quickest route to satisfactory solutions.

"Move," he bit out more loudly. Dealing with these dipshit reporters wasted time he didn't have. A child was dead, for God's sake. They needed answers ASAP.

Unexpected images from the time surrounding his son's death attacked his mind with strobe-light speed. A final wheeze of breath. Unnatural stillness. The scent of incense at the funeral. York fisted his hands, fingernails digging into his palms.

Danny.

He thrust his hands into his pockets, mentally slamming his son's memory back into its box. That had been another life. Another ambition. Another person. Since Danny's death, York had taken strong measures to avoid cases like this, even going so far as requesting Avery keep him off the death investigations pertaining to children. Yet, here he was, right in the thick of one. Assigned to work with a GEI geneticist to uncover the truth.

A tall reporter, his expression aggressive, tried to block York. "I heard it was the child. Was she in an accident?"

"Take it somewhere else." York gave the man a chance to comply before he tore the Tracer controller, branded with the *Chicago Times* logo, from the guy's hands and flung it. Above, a single drone spiraled out of the pack, plummeted, and crashed into the courtyard's sleek marble fountain.

"Hey!" With a searing glare, the reporter lunged forward. "Lieutenant"—the guy dipped his gaze to read York's ID—"Richmond." He stepped back. "Whose side are you on?"

"The child's." Why did people always reduce genetic issues to *our* side versus *their* side? The shadow of a beard and a slightly darker expression told York that, like himself, the reporter was a Coder. The man was also sturdy and muscular. York forced calm as his instincts prickled. He glanced about.

"Wait… Richmond. Isn't your mother one of the leaders of the anti-GEI movement?" one reporter asked.

The other reporters closed ranks like ants after a legs-up beetle. They spit out question after question.

"Is it true a GEI child died?"

"Isn't that unheard of for Artificial Womb Engineered babies?"

"Can you give us a name? A quote?"

"From which generation? C? D?"

"What does Fredrick B-Gastion have to do with this?"

York felt his spine tighten one vertebra at a time. He lowered a shoulder, then shoved the tall reporter out of the way, ready to linebacker a path to the air-car if necessary.

Central in his mind, though, were the words *why* and *how*.

Why B-Gastion's child and how had this happened?

Vi grabbed a fistful of the back of his shirt. She pulled him to her, saying under her breath, "Easy, York. Captain will be pissed if we're on the twenty-four-hour news."

He twisted around to glare. "Don't give a shit."

"Well, you better."

She was right. He fought his anger, sucking in a deep breath. With his steely gaze fixed on the reporters, he said, "You'll know when we know." To Vi, he muttered, "Happy?"

She gave him a smart-ass smile. Her light brown hair was cut in the latest style—short on one side, then angled down and around to almost brush her shoulder on the other. Her appearance was sharp, like a person who had it together, but she seemed tired. Her green eyes locked on his a second too long, and he glimpsed sadness. Like him, she'd lost a kid after trying some newfangled genetic-enhancement crap. God, if Vi could keep it together while working a case like this, he damn well had to.

He turned his attention to the reporter in the front of the pack. Setting his jaw and fisting his hands, York stared the reporter down until the guy stepped back, creating an opening.

"Let's go." York gestured for Vi to step through the line.

They'd no sooner made it to the air-car before his QuL trilled again. This time, the call was from B-Gastion, asking York if he would personally monitor events at the morgue.

B-Gastion had come to York's aide when he'd been desperate to find help for his son and no one else had given a damn. Now it was time to repay his debt.

He closed his eyes. "Of course. It would be an honor."

When Kindra arrived at Seville, she surged through the door of the spacious laboratory. Late, in a lousy mood, and worried about Brianna's unusual outburst. As she traveled the hallway, the nursery room caught her attention. Peering through the glass windows at the rows and rows of artificial wombs, she sighed, struggling to calm her nerves. At a station at the left, technicians took the genetically modified embryos—the ones she had designed to fit the Committee requirements—and placed them in wombs where they would grow until full term. She thought of all the parents who waited expectantly for their baby. She recalled the foreign yet wonderful feeling she'd had when she'd held Brianna for the first.

Perfection. This was how it should be. She moved on to her office, then dropped her satchel on the curved table that had alternating glass partitions separating the work and comfort stations. Automatically, she took her lab coat off its customary hook and shrugged it on.

An unfamiliar baritone penetrated her thoughts. "I'm looking for Dr. B-Zaika."

Glancing across the room, she froze as she spotted her lab assistant directing a deeply tanned, rock-solid man her way. She had less than a second to scrutinize the stranger: Coder race, dark hair, shadow of beard, and oozing an air of mystery.

He turned toward her, and her knees nearly buckled under the onslaught of his gaze. Exotic and unfamiliar energy fired through her. Being GEI, she was used to perfection. And since she worked at the top genetic lab surrounded by some of the greatest GEI minds in the world, it took a lot to knock her off-kilter. But there was something compelling about this Coder.

In a few great strides, he left B-Watson and crossed the distance between them to stand inches away. His earthy male scent fascinated her—a paradox, considering the near-lethal accusation in his black-brown eyes.

He looked…angry. She retreated a step, then realized her mistake. He eased closer, and she stared up at him.

"Dr. B-Zaika?" He lifted a thick, raven-black eyebrow.

"Yes. How can I help you?"

Did she know this man? She didn't think so. But the intensity of his gaze suggested *he* knew *her*. She peered past his broad shoulders to where Harry hurried to catch up.

"This is Lieutenant York Richmond, Chicago PD," Harry B-Watson said when he reached them.

An invisible capsule of tension crackled around them. Lieutenant Richmond offered her a tight nod. Police didn't frequent genetics centers. What was going on?

Her anxiety escalated with his silent, critical glare. Did she measure up? No, she didn't think so. Different standards. He was of the Coder race—people who descended organically from one generation to the next as far back as the beginning of time. The foolish debate regarding gene manipulation raging between his people and her own GEI race had been going on forever. Still, Kindra got the impression the cosmic heat shield of hostility he emanated arose from far more than basic ideological differences. Somehow, this was…personal for him.

"You're the genetics specialist?"

"Yes." She put on a winning smile, then turned to B-Watson. "Is the Samuel Experiment complete yet?"

He indicated it was not, then trotted off. The clack of his shoes echoed in the cavernous lab. Good or bad, she didn't want her assistant meddling in whatever the police were here for.

She faced the handsome lieutenant. "It's most unusual to have a detective visit Seville. What brings you here?"

"I've been instructed to escort you to the Lakeshore District morgue."

Her stomach flipped before making a hard landing. Not in a million years would she have expected that. "The morgue? Why would I need—"

"Tell me about D-Generation," he cut in.

A prickle of fear skated along her spine. "D-Generation?"

Brianna. She resisted the urge to scream. *Is my baby okay?* Tension darted through her, out of control. When she finally looked him in the eye, he stared at her as if anticipating more information.

"Yes, D," he said.

She drew in a calming breath, forcing composure to overrule her shaken nerves. *Be reasonable.* In an instant, she could display the top-secret details on the overhead instructional computer.

"Perhaps I should check with—"

"I have the required authority," he said.

"Secure ID level?"

"Yes." He sighed impatiently. "Crescent M."

She should ask him for his credentials. Kindra eyed him, hesitant, then shrugged, deciding he'd earned the lightning version at least. "The main difference between C and D-Generations is the Committee narrowed the physical choices—"

"Incredible how you scientists keep doing that." He uttered *scientists* as though it were a filthy occupation.

She ignored his tone. "And they increased the intellectual potential by three standard deviations."

"Oh, Jesus."

"These children are beyond genius level." Kindra smiled, thinking of her own daughter, then reminded herself she'd better find out what this was all about. She could think of only one reason to visit a morgue. "Why are genetics of interest to you, Lieutenant?"

"There's been a D-Generation death."

"An accident?" She struggled to conceal her distress.

"No. Not that we can tell." His gaze homed in on her. "We don't have answers yet. But we need to start with natural causes."

"That's impossible. Why, a D-Generation child would be no more than—"

"Two. The girl would have been three in a few weeks." His jaw tensed, creating a chain reaction of muscles rippling to his dark brow. "A prominent and very distraught family is insisting on an investigation. It's a requirement, regardless. These things aren't supposed to happen."

"No. No, they're not." A rush of relief filled her lungs. Thank God it wasn't *her* little girl. At once, a rain of guilt drowned the thought. Somewhere in the city, another mother had to be inconsolable.

In the past, Kindra may not have reacted so powerfully. Somehow, motherhood had opened a depth of emotion inside her. She'd seen the shift happen with other GEIs when children entered their lives, but she'd never expected to feel it herself.

Kindra felt the blood drain from her face, and her

pulse raced. *Stay professional.* "Computer, the D-Generation design, please." Raising her hand, she directed the officer's attention to the holographic screen at the end of the room. "Take a look, Lieutenant. Ds are expected to have an average life span of one hundred and sixty years."

"Holy sh—"

A ribbon of pride danced through her at his amazement. Genetic engineering had changed the course of history. GEIs were the product of the twenty-first century's California quest for cosmetic perfectionism—the ideal body, complexion, hair, and eyes. Then intellect became a hot commodity. Now, people could purchase it—and even change it—for the right price, including perfect children comprised of features chosen from an enhancement catalog. *Designer babies*, some called them. York was correct—her people simply didn't die. Not until the brain gave out. That was the one thing they couldn't clone. A sister facility of the Seville worked on cloning body parts, and her fellow scientists constantly developed and refined techniques to increase the speed at which they could grow body parts.

On some gut level, Kindra detested the idea her parents had created her as part of a fad for perfection and beauty, though she couldn't blast the benefits of an increased life span with immunity to all known illnesses. It seemed most other people appreciated the advantage of that sort of manipulation, too—even Coders. The days of cancer and disease were behind them, and that was a far more important outcome than simply being pretty.

She lifted a holograph pad from the desk, then plopped it back. Information about germ lines and stem and somatic cells scrolled across the enormous display. She hugged herself, trying to still a sudden sense of unease.

What had caused the child's death? Had she been murdered? Or was there an undetected mistake in the genetics? Would such a mistake be present in all

D-Generation children, or could the error be restricted to the one deceased child? Kindra forced herself not to jump to conclusions while tempering her urge to analyze. Minor tweaks in the genome could produce major changes. This turn of events gave her even more reasons to urge for a delay in the E-Generation release. In her estimation, they were moving too far, too fast. She knew what was at stake. And she knew who they would blame if something went awry—*her*.

An almost overwhelming feeling of powerlessness and guilt came over her. Kindra couldn't help but wonder if she had done something to contribute to the unknown little girl's death. She could only imagine how she'd feel if something happened to her child. She glanced sideways at the lieutenant, pushing the thought aside.

Evidence. That was what she needed. No sense getting worked up without the facts.

Lieutenant Richmond studied the screen, and she observed him. His unruly eyebrows furrowed above intense dark eyes. Short wisps of hair curled past the clean neckline of his blue shirt. She blinked, lacing her fingers together. He, no doubt, had too much hair—an unpleasant trait of Coders, with their unkempt shadow beards. GEIs hadn't been engineered to have facial hair. Only smooth perfection. Even so, she wondered how his hair would feel. Soft? Springy? Coarse? A curious knot tightened in her chest.

Unfolding her arms, she drew her attention to the screen and the data she knew by rote. It was information she'd learned at her father's knee. Robert A-Zaika had always found time to answer her questions, always encouraged her, always had confidence in her. On a heavy sigh, she resolved to keep her emotions in check. This wasn't about her parents.

When the data ceased flickering over the display, Lieutenant Richmond shifted toward her with an unexpected look of…admiration?

"You understand that?"

Kindra gave an abrupt nod. Few people saw what she did as anything special. "I'll need to examine the girl, run tests, and meet with the medical examiner. But I have a petition I'm scheduled to present to the Committee in…" She checked the clock on the table. "Oh my. Ten minutes. I can't leave until I'm finished with that."

York crossed his arms over his chest. "What could be so important? Doesn't it bother you a child has died?"

"Of course it does."

"Then reschedule the meeting."

Kindra hesitated. "It's not that easy."

"It would be if it were *your* child."

Inhaling sharply, she pressed her lips together. "There's nothing I can do for that child now. But my report could influence the quality of life for millions of people in the next generation, so you're welcome to wait here until I'm done, or I can meet you at the morgue."

His jaw firm, he bit out, "I'll wait."

She snatched the computer key for her presentation from the desk. "Suit yourself."

To her irritation, he followed a few steps behind her. At first, she thought he was going to hang out in the outer office, but he stayed with her as she moved into the hall. What was with this guy? She clenched her teeth in annoyance, but then immediately imagined the way her father used to tap her jawline to break her of the habit.

On a long, slow exhale, she tried to focus on the major points of her presentation and ignore Lieutenant Richmond, hoping he'd give up and go away. If she didn't know better, she'd think he considered her a flight risk.

As she navigated the halls to the conference room, a door suddenly opened. A technician darted out, forcing Kindra and York to stop short. Kindra shifted her gaze to the slowly closing door, peeking inside. Lights glowed in a dim blueish hue. She could see the Artificial Wombs lined up in rows. It had been a long while since she'd ventured there. Not since before Brianna was born.

In a flash of memory, she considered the way GEI children were conceived and born. Usually, the mature egg and sperm were retrieved from the prospective parents, combined in the lab, then genetically altered according to the parents' choices selected from a list of attributes dictated by the Committee. Viable unions were implanted into an Artificial Womb to grow and mature until gestation was complete.

Kindra caught the lieutenant's gaze also locked on the room. His face darkened, perhaps because he didn't approve of the birth method. Most Coders didn't. For GEI, it was simply the way it was done, as opposed to the Coder's, who propagated through intercourse.

One thing both groups shared, though, was there were no unwanted children in this day and age. Birth control had moved far beyond accidental pregnancies. All children were wanted, except for the ones the Committee deemed imperfect.

Kindra stopped outside the conference room door. Anxiety squeezed her stomach, and the leaden ball that had been her breakfast moved higher into her chest. Her heart raced. "You can't go in. Wait here."

AVAILABLE NOW

Read on for a sneak peek of *Awakening Fire.*

You met Seth in *Forever at Risk*
Now see him where his legacy on earth began in

AWAKENING FIRE
THE DIVINE TREE GUARDIAN SERIES

LARISSA EMERALD

 Prologue

Isle of Skye, Scotland
1120 AD

The crusty old man with long ropes of coal-black hair didn't look like an angel, but he had earned the attention of Venn and his eleven brothers. With a flick of the wrist, the angel plucked an enormous boulder into the air and dropped it on the snarling barghest, plastering the demon onto the ground.

"Guid God, that was close." Minutes ago, he'd thought he and his brothers would all be dead as, in force, they'd fought against the barthest that had attacked them from out of nowhere. Then that angel had joined their ranks and outdone them all. With heaving breaths, Venn crouched near the fire pit and thrust his sword into the flames. As the beast's thick, yellow blood sizzled on the metal, Venn's brothers gathered in a loose semicircle: Njorth, Ian, Euler,

Rurik, Aidan, Brandt, Colby, Graham, Dustin, Tristan, Lachlan. All alive. Bruised, bloodied, clothing clawed and shredded. But alive. Thanks be to God.

Seth, as the angel called himself, perched atop the sandstone rock, apparently fishing dirt from under his fingernails. Beneath him, the boulder flattened the malicious barghest facedown into the dirt, limbs and head protruding, far larger than the biggest dog Venn had ever seen. A foul odor of rotten eggs permeated the air as the thing fought mightily against the stone's weight. The barghest scored the earth with four-inch claws, flashed fangs the length of swords, and snarled.

Venn coughed at the stench, then winced as a biting pain seized his rib.

"Finish off the monster," Njorth, the eldest brother, demanded.

"Nay." Seth breathed deeply. His wings expanded and retracted in time with each inhalation. "Io will not die this day. My brother is cast into a net by his own feet." With one hand reaching skyward, he summoned a somewhat smaller boulder at cliff's edge, which he dropped on the barghest's protruding head. "That may silence him for a while."

The rasp in the angel's voice brought to mind wheels catching on rough ground. "'Tis said that each man's future is written before it occurs." Seth passed his perceptive gaze over the brothers. When he came to Venn, his expression darkened, his eyes narrowed. "And 'tis true. Well, partially so. Occasional exceptions have been known to alter one's course. Brothers, you have been chosen."

Venn stood, met the angel's piercing blue stare, and sheathed his sword. A biting wind scurried along the embankment at his back, then shot out over the cliff to meet the riotous waves, enhancing the swirl and shift of the late-morning fog.

The brothers were border guards, protecting their kin

against skirmishes and raiding. Venn had been the last invited to this gathering, most likely due to his fierce disbelief in angels.

Not anymore.

"The two prime virtues ascribed to Highlanders are fidelity and courage. This day thou art offered a great challenge to draw on both of these merits." Seth glanced to the enormous tree several rods from the brothers as he circled his hand upward in a dramatic flourish.

The undercurrent in the air changed, foretelling an approaching storm. The ground shook with an intensity that sent Venn tumbling to the dirt. He rolled sideways to avoid the fire but still fell close enough to it to singe his hair. The pungent burned smell pinched his nose. He staggered to his feet.

As he got his bearings and raised his head, a tremendous sound akin to a ship splitting in half thundered painfully through his ears and chest. The tree rose, uprooted like God himself had reached down and plucked it from the earth. Soil and rocks dropped away, and Venn shifted his stance, muscles tensed, as his fight-or-flight instinct warred within.

Suspended in midair a furlong overhead, the tree began to rotate. Agonizingly slow, at first, then faster and faster, gaining momentum. Clumps of earth flew from the roots as a rain of rock and mud pelted the ground. Within the space of a few breaths, the oak created a whirl of limbs and branches, and leaves peeled away. Venn recoiled, shielding his eyes, as a burst of white light and a deafening boom pummeled them all. He glanced up in time to glimpse the trunk splintering apart, chunks of tree launching skyward and soaring across the land in every direction.

And then it was gone.

The maelstrom was over as quickly as it had begun, and twelve forked sticks dropped at Seth's feet. Venn cursed under his breath and palmed his bearded face. What had they just witnessed?

He sprinted toward Njorth and clasped his elder brother's arm, ready to drag him away from the alleged angel.

Seth shot him a reproachful glare, then knelt to retrieve the sticks. "Peace!" He tossed one to each of the twelve brothers, saving Venn for last.

Venn had not intended to comply with the angel's bidding, but he caught the stick instinctively. As soon as his hand closed around the rough wood, an odd burning sensation spread under his skin, followed by pain slicing through him from neck to groin.

What had the angel done?

A pleased, knowing smile broke across Seth's face as spasms continued twisting in Venn's chest. He groaned, hearing his brothers do the same. He turned to find their heads thrown back, their arms spread wide, all seeming to be experiencing the same horror he was.

The sequence coursed through Venn three agonizing times. When the fit subsided, he gasped airless pants as if he'd raced across several deep furrows.

Seth's smile vanished. "For every honest man bent to the purpose of noble deeds, there are thousands driven by greed, lust, revenge, and power. Hundreds vying for the secrets of youth, the secrets of the universe, the secrets to manipulating time and space. Men whose misplaced allegiance increases evil."

Venn balanced the stick in his palm and tested its weight, curiosity replacing his agony. Oddly heavy, it felt like part of him, an extension of his arm.

"The Divine Tree has splintered and will take root in new domains. Thou hast been given a divining rod to direct you to your tree. As Immortal Guardians, you are to protect that tree and its secrets with your life. But most importantly...do not allow the Dark Realm entry into the tree. And if your tree dies, so shall you. And all of humanity will suffer the consequences for the loss of its knowledge. Go, and be well."

As if that explained everything, Seth disintegrated into shimmering particles that faded to nothing.

"Wait," Venn called. Immortal Guardians? Tales of Odin and Yggdrasill and the Christian uprising vied in a mist of confusion.

Why would Venn and his brothers be called to guard anything? Seth must be mad.

Venn tossed the divining rod aside. "Firewood," he scoffed.

When he looked up, he met his brothers' disapproving stares as they gathered their belongings. Njorth prodded his injured thigh, where an ugly gash oozed red. He grimaced, raised and lowered his leg. Then the wound dried up and closed.

His eyes widened. "Look at that. Healed." He turned to his brothers, each of them looking in turn to see the cut now gone. He gave a small chuckle. "Oh, but it aches like hell."

"Stop complaining," their brother Ian grumbled.

Njorth gave Venn a hearty clap on the shoulder, a wallop meant to suffice for a long time. "This ain't half-bad."

They were *immortal*? No, it wasn't possible.

Part of him wanted to ignore Seth's directives as nonsense and head home, but he stole another glance at Njorth's healed thigh. He eyed his other brothers, packed and ready, each fisting their shares of the tree. He swallowed, pulling a sheepskin pouch over his shoulder as his heartbeat escalated with indecision, then slowed in resignation.

Ah, hell, brothers fought side by side. He trod toward the fire pit to retrieve his divining rod from where he'd thrown it. As he fisted the wood, a prickling force pulsed up into his arm and shoulder, the rod seeming to yank him to the east. He shook off the feeling, his attention was forced back to the barghest, whose menacing paws thrashed from beneath the boulders, announcing that its wild nature had revived.

"I can't stand that beast," Euler declared. He raised his sword, stepping closer to Io. "Let's take his head and be done with him while we can."

"No." Seth's booming voice crashed over them like a rolling wave.

"Hope he stays under there 'til he rots," Njorth grumbled.

Venn backed cautiously away, a hand on his sword hilt, allowing a wide berth for the beast's vicious claws. "Let's go. I suggest we figure out the game rules somewhere else. Before we hav'ta yield more of our blood."

1

Present Day

At the subterranean entrance to the Divine Tree sanctuary, Venn Hearst halted and raised his eyes to the etchings of a wolf and hawk emblazoned in the aged wood above the door, a nod to his alternate forms. Venn extended his tattooed wrist, positioning the elaborately inked tree, and the pulsing artery beneath it, below a glistening twisted root for the anointing ritual. An amber-colored drop of sap spilled over the image, then pooled and bubbled before it was absorbed into his skin, sending a sharp zing to each of his neurons before settling within the larger matching tat on his back.

The language of the universe rustled through the air. The Secrets men died to know, Guardians swore to protect, and the Dark Realms were determined to steal or destroy were housed within this sacred place.

His Divine Tree was one of the original dozen hidden around the globe. There were eleven left after the Divine Tree Guardians had lost his brother Tristan along with the Divine Tree in Germany in the mid-nineteen hundreds. The tree's demise had caused the earth to shift on its axis ever so slightly, bringing them one step closer to Armageddon with an escalation of malevolent forces. Evil had blossomed with Hitler taking millions of lives before balance could be restored. It had been an uphill battle ever since.

Venn opened and closed his fist, considering the tattoo on his wrist. Not even one more tree could be lost.

"Benison," the oak whispered.

"Blessings," Venn returned. "My strength and loyalty are yours."

With his vow, the door to the tree creaked opened, and he strode through the massive entry. He looked around the comfortable aboveground chambers and kept walking. Keeping watch wasn't his intention this night. No, he sought the tombs within the root structure below and hoped the tree would communicate to him if something out of the ordinary was happening.

He grabbed a nearby flashlight from the alcove next to the door, flipped it on, and started along the narrow tunneled path, down a staircase that had been fashioned by twisted knots of wood and roots fused together over centuries. It wound deep into the layers of knowledge, to the catacomb of interconnected scripts, like a true, living computer.

Once in the belly, he ran a hand over an electrical switch. Battery powered lights illuminate the cave-like room in a pale glow. Venn glanced about and drew an awed breath. *Holy shit. The place had grown.*

With careful steps, he moved from the tunnel into a cavern, where rough splinters jutted out of smooth swirls in the timber's pattern, creating a golden wooden cave. He used to come down here often in the beginning, during the early years of loneliness, always expecting to discover something exceptional. Which he usually did.

He'd learned that if he pricked himself on this special wood, a series of images would fire though his brain, teaching him something new, its lessons sharper and more thorough than those of any history or science channel on TV.

Centuries ago, he'd stumbled on this cavern and its amazing phenomenon quite by accident. The power the tree gave him had become an obsession, the data exchange an addiction. He knew better than to come back again after that. But this time he had no choice, his duty demanded he use every means available to him. He was well aware of the risks and didn't intend to overstep his limits.

Something was off-kilter in the universe, and he needed to know why. The odd weather pattern—winter when it should be spring—was an ominous sign, Venn knew, even if humans simply took it as a fluke of nature. Just as humans showed symptoms of illness, so too did the machinations of the universe. And a shift between good and evil often triggered such nasty weather patterns.

He needed to be on high alert. "Custos," he spoke quietly to the ancient tree. "Do you know what's going on?"

There was no answer.

Taking a seat in a worn cradle of wood, he felt the need to connect with the Divine Tree…and to his brothers. He squeezed the back of his neck. Perhaps that's what the problem was. Not outside at all, but within him.

He felt as isolated from everything as this tree was. What was it like to house all humanity but not feel humanity?

The groan and creak of the tree, as if it were caught by a strong gust of wind, caused Venn to lift his head. Seth stood framed in the tunnel doorway. "I didn't think you'd be down here," the angel said, walking into the chamber.

Now Venn *knew* there was trouble brewing. The angel rarely dropped in just to say hello. "What's happenin'?" Venn asked in way of greeting.

Seth shrugged, his wings lifting and falling with the movement. "I'm not sure. But you must feel it also if you're down here."

"Indeed. Have a seat," Venn motioned to another curve of wood.

Seth sat and crossed his legs, resting his back and folded wings against the smooth inner walls of the tree. "I dunno. On one hand the off weather pattern seems like a trivial thing, but coupled with all the unrest in the world—with ISIS beheading people in the Middle East and people protesting over police in the US—I think we need to pay close attention."

"I agree. The planet is digressing into a state of anarchy and I'd bet my right arm that the Dark Realm is behind it all," Venn proclaimed.

"No doubt."

"I think you'd better hang around," Venn suggested.

"Fine. You got a room to spare?" Seth asked, firing a glance from beneath heavy eyelids without lifting his head.

"No."

Seth shrugged. "Then I can't help you."

Venn chuckled, knowing full well he'd just gained a house guest. "It's hard to think back to when this guardianship began." He rested his head back and closed his eyes, trying to see that far into the past. "You know you could have given us a little more information when you set us on this task."

"What for? You figured it out."

"Huh. It took me forever to learn to control my shifting. The hawk being able to manipulate time and space, and the wolf's incredible strength. Shit, I was a mess in those days."

"You're still a mess," Seth said with exaggerated distain.

Venn straightened. "Hey, I didn't ask for this gig. You can head back up anytime."

Emma sympathized with anyone who had to make transatlantic flights on a regular basis. The trip from Paris to Atlanta's Hartsfield-Jackson airport had left her weary as a rag doll. Two hours later, she was still stifling yawns as she surveyed the snow-covered park where her mélange-metal statue would reside.

"I'm sorry. I shouldn't have made you stop here on the way from the airport. You must be exhausted." Grams tugged the zipper of her trendy black leather jacket higher before passing the leash attached to her little, aging Yorkshire terrier, Izzy, from one hand to the other. The pup scooted around her legs. "It was thoughtless of me. I'm just so excited."

Emma shrugged. "I'm fine," she assured her grandmother, then twisted to face the trunk of the enormous tree they stood beneath when the next yawn came. A whisper of energy coiled around her, heat seeming to seep out of the bark itself. She pursed her mouth and clasped her arms around her rib cage. As if the move offered any protection. Fatigue always made her paranoid. She even sometimes saw visions, though she didn't like to admit it, even to herself.

She sighed. No use in worrying about something she couldn't control, and she'd long since learned she wasn't in the driver's seat where her visions were concerned. Instead, she engaged in her most prevalent form of evasion, her art.

Nothing wrong with burying problems in a little work.

She studied the space again. Which metals would capture the hues of oyster shells in the sky? What subject would best fit the colors? Emma jotted down some mental notes for her next project. She watched the changing colors of dusk descend on the park as clouds loomed, back-lit in an eerie coppery shimmer. The diffused light made the snow appear almost warm, the rocks somehow spongy, and the trees… They were mystical.

Her apprehension escalated as the walkway in front of her blurred. Her knees grew weak.

No. Not this time.

She sucked in a deep breath and tensed, resisting. But she knew with sickening certainty that the vision was coming. There was no controlling it…

An arrow shaft protruded from her chest, and air wheezed through her stagnant lungs. In the wake of the brutal, radiating pain, time slowed. Her heart stopped.

Oh God.

An image of a huge gray wolf materialized, howling a cry of grief alongside her lifeless body, and it lingered, dimming slowly to a sepia shadow. Had she…died here?

Emma blinked, disoriented, as the brief manifestation faded, reality setting back in. Exhaling hard, she shifted her feet, peering down at her strappy, crystal-embellished, leopard-print sandals and seeking solid ground. Izzy licked at her toes where they peeked from her shoes, as if trying to console her as best he could.

Her gaze swept up her own body, and she settled shaky fingers over her beating heart. No blood. No arrow. Definitely alive.

Still, the suffocating sensation of a collapsed lung remained, causing her stomach to churn. How she even knew what one felt like alarmed her.

Stop thinking about it.

With determined strength, Emma overcame the pervasive mental intrusion, forcing her attention back to the grossly neglected Georgia park where she stood trembling, to the place her sculpture would call home.

She'd had these dreams and visions her whole life, and when she'd researched the phenomenon, she'd discovered they were each giving her a glimpse of one of her past lives. If one believed in that sort of thing. Which she did. But knowing that didn't make it any less disturbing.

Emma's breath swirled in a misty cloud as she focused on her surroundings. Cold, damp air patted her cheeks. The massive oak before her released a sad moan. Or was that just her active imagination at work? Whatever it was triggered a familiar warmth that spread into her limbs, and reminded her she possessed…talents beyond her visions. Heat radiated through her right arm, and she glanced down, opening her blazing hot fist to discover she'd inadvertently melted her grandmother's butterfly key fob beyond recognition.

Some *talents*. More like she'd been cursed.

With an unsteady sigh, she pushed her hair away from her face. Geez, her life hadn't changed one iota. Since she was a toddler, she'd been molding metal with her bare hands as if it were clay, both intentionally and accidentally. It was the latter that caused her grief. The episode with a neighborhood boy and his squished red Hot Wheels car came to mind. It always did. Her dad had been so angry with her.

"Are you okay?"

Her grandmother's question snapped her back to the present. Would Grams know if she lied? She'd discovered when she'd moved to New York that the visions and dreams had lessened with the distance. She'd run all the way to Paris to avoid them. And they must have let go, too, because she hadn't thought of them for a long, long while.

"Sure. But I can't say the same for this." She dangled the key chain in the air.

Her grandmother gave a chuckle. "I should have nicknamed you Hot Hands."

Emma managed to summon a smile, but it faltered as her gaze shifted back to that tree. Its spindly canopy of branches seemed to reach out. The hair on her arms prickled. Something in the fractures of time yanked free and another ripple of unease washed over her.

Good and evil used this place as a playground. At the moment, evil acted the bully. She felt a bizarre tug-of-war for dominance, the power of it making her sway.

Leave. Me. Alone.

This evening's vision was beyond vivid—a seven-point-five on the Richter scale, and it wasn't passing as it normally did. She flailed her arms, trying to shake off her frustration. She usually had an easier time coming out of it. An erratic pulse thumped in her neck, bringing her circulation back. Her temples ached with the awakening.

She shook her head. *Ignore. Regroup. Move on.*

Thank goodness her grandmother, who tarried a few steps behind, wouldn't know the depth of Emma's latest episode, since time distorted or elongated only within her mind. What she needed was an anchor, physically and mentally. There was no way she'd allow her father to be right about her differences making her crazy. She didn't have a psychotic disorder as he'd suggested when she was young. No, she would control the lapse, but, darn, this bout threatened her common sense. She'd never seen herself die before.

Besides, wasn't that supposed to kill you or something?

Or was that just in dreams, not visions? She gave a mental shrug, figuring it didn't matter because she had both.

Focus. She was here on a job. The park.

It was spring in Tyler, Georgia, yet the late-season snow masked the evidence. Weeds and yellow wildflowers nudged aside a layer of snow, and fresh green growth attempted to unfurl on branches. The square must have been lovely at one time, especially when everything began to bloom, but not now. A battered, rotten wood bench lay on the ground sideways, collapsed. The sidewalk that wound through the center of the park resembled a war zone, with chunks of concrete broken and upended. The branches of the old oak swept the earth. Clearly ignored for many, many years, the mammoth tree looked as if it had never been pruned or shaped.

The untamed tree was so out-of-character for prim-and-proper Georgia. Just like her. Her dad had always proclaimed that her overactive imagination would lead to trouble. If he only knew the whole truth.

A hand slid across Emma's back and bony fingers grasped her shoulder. She almost jumped out of her grandmother's hug.

"Just think, a Grant getting the honor of creating a statue for the old town square. I can hardly believe it." Grams heaved one of her exaggerated, bursting-with-pride sighs, the way she did when the family dinner table was landscaped to perfection.

"You drive a hard bargain, Grams. The committee couldn't say no." And neither could Emma. Her grandmother had requested a sculpture of a confederate soldier on a rearing horse. Not very original, but Emma obliged, thankful for both the much-needed income and the chance to build her portfolio. She gradually relaxed into the woman's solid embrace, somewhat grounded again.

She touched her head to her grandmother's salon-teased auburn one, in the same let's-stick-together way she'd done since she was six, when she'd spent every summer vacation here after her family had moved to New York.

"Thanks for your help," Emma said. Nothing like getting paid to visit her favorite relative. Since the city had commissioned her sculpture for the park renovation project, she'd be hanging out for the next few weeks to supervise its placement and participate in the dedication ceremony.

Grams nodded. "Anytime. Paris is too darn far away, if you ask me." She picked Izzy up and tucked him beneath her arm.

Actually, the greater distance meant fewer visions, so it wasn't even far enough. Emma wasn't sure why, but they seemed to be worse, more frequent, when she returned to her Georgia birthplace. Bonus points for Paris.

"We talk and Skype all the time," Emma pointed out.

"That's not the same as seeing your smiling face." Her grandmother slid a hand down Emma's arm and back up over her shoulder. "Look at you. You're shivering."

Ominous gray clouds were moving in, and the sky was growing darker. Emma felt more than saw the clump of wet red clay that oozed into her Sam Edelman sandals. She tamped her foot against a rock to clear it. "What an awful spring. Can't believe it snowed on Easter."

"Yes. The pecan blooms froze. The crop'll be ruined." A smile lit Grams's eyes, and she tsked, seeming to dismiss the unfortunate prediction that might steal her pocket money. "But give it a few days. It'll warm up."

"I'll hold you to that."

Tree branches whipped one way, then the other, generating an eerie whistling. Emma shuddered, then tugged the neckline of her suddenly constricting turtleneck sweater as she turned to explore a staked-out plot of ground. "It looks like this is where they plan to put the statue."

Her gaze swept along the snow-patched ground, up the broken walkway, to the side of the park where fluorescent-orange construction fencing sectioned off individual trees, marking them for protection. Landscaping equipment near the road formed a neat line, ready to be put to use.

A tiny ping caught in her gut, and her internal compass gravitated to the old oak standing center stage. Its trunk stretched out to the size of a small house, as if several trees had grown together. She frowned as intense golden eyes seemed to peer at her from the grained bark. A figment of her imagination? With her history, it had to be.

When the eyes vanished, she angled her head, unable to shake the weird drag on her heart. As if she should know something important, yet couldn't bring it forth. The feeling didn't seem like a remnant of her vision but felt like it originated from an entirely different source. More like an unfathomable power or presence. She scanned the park and rubbed her chilled arms, but she didn't see a single soul.

Io slipped behind the downed bulldozer bucket, in predator mode, his eyes fixed on his target: Emma Grant. The machine inched to the side as his back jammed against a metal support. In his eagerness, he hadn't sufficiently controlled his brute strength. He grumbled at the oversight but kept tuned to the young woman. While in human form, as he was now, his senses were faulty. It was a weak form, practically useless, with few special powers.

He'd known the moment Emma Grant had set foot on Georgia soil.

Not such a difficult task, really. He'd been expecting her.

Now, he was curious about the reason she'd stopped at the park on her way from the airport. Was the Divine Tree's power already blooming in Emma? Had the old tree spoken to her?

He'd met her quite by accident years ago when she was a little girl of five. They were in an ice cream shop and he'd accidently dropped a handful of coins on the floor—as fine motor skills was another issue he had with the human form. But it turned into a fortunate event for him, really, for Emma gathered the coins up off the floor. And to her great embarrassment, when she handed them back to him the lot was fused together in a solid clump of metal.

He knew then and there that she was gifted. And he made it his business to discover why. Eavesdropping in on her dreams at night gave him the connection to her past. Even over the years after she moved from Tyler, he managed to keep track of her. He was damned proud of himself for discovering the reason behind her metal-altering ability.

Well, it wasn't precisely *his* discovery, but he would take credit for it nonetheless.

When he'd killed Emma in her past life and she'd lain on the grassy ground with his arrow jutting out of her chest, her blood had seeped into this magical oak's roots. Who knew such a simple act would create the catalyst to destroy a Divine Tree? He certainly hadn't. Not until the High Counsel of Devils had recently congratulated him for it, that is. And he wasn't disappointed.

That arrow, her blood, and her reincarnation had caused a shift, something even he couldn't grasp the implications of. It had taken him shitloads of long, painful, boring hours of watching before he discovered how he could use her newborn alchemist powers to his advantage. He deserved this boon, and the recognition from the counsel. He'd show his brother, Seth, that he was equally as favored by his superiors.

Now if only he could overcome the free will part of the equation. He couldn't force her into using her alchemist powers on the metal as he wanted her to. At least not physically.

But there were other ways to get the results he desired.

With a mental shake, he glared at Emma.

Did she realize the connection she shared with the tree? If so, he'd have to move much quicker than he'd thought. No, no, he wouldn't allow things to get out of hand. He swiped a restless hand along his jaw.

He tried to quiet the nervous energy that continually tugged him in conflicting directions. One moment he was certain of his mission's success, the next of its failure. His gaze darted from Emma to Mrs. Busybody, listening intently. He plunged his hands into his pockets, withdrew them, then clasped them behind him.

The best he could determine, Emma was simply cold, not agitated or suspicious.

And Mrs. Grant took credit for arranging the commission of the statue her granddaughter had arrived to install.

Yes, it was better that Emma thought her grandmother was the instigator. Better she not discover the significance of the invitation to the installation ceremony. At least not until the ruination of the tree was complete or Emma and the Guardian were dead. Either outcome would give him great pleasure.

After all, he'd discovered firsthand that the best way to make someone suffer was to destroy the one thing that someone most loved. Yes, revenge would be his. About time.

Seth, Mr. Goodie-Goodie, would soon have his world turned upside down. And Venn and the Divine Tree along with him. He could barely contain his excitement. Three for the price of one. Brilliant.

Excited and restless, Io tugged on his shirt sleeve, then sought focus by touching the picture of a burned tree he kept tucked in his pocket. It represented his brother's failure. His channeled hatred grew and his smokescreen, the shield he'd put in place so the tree wouldn't detect his presence, disintegrated. Damn.

The stupid dog in the old ladies arms barked and growled.

A deep moan resounded within the catacomb. *Custos?* Venn straightened from his relaxed position. Immediately, his attention shot upward—above him, outside—and he stood.

What *was* that?

An irresistible tug made him palm his chest. He proceeded through the cavern entrance, back up the knotted stairs and angled tunnel, the pull intensifying with each step. If he were human, he'd be wondering if he were having a heart attack.

He hadn't felt this collision of energy in two centuries.

Inside the sprawling tree, he climbed rough-hewn stairs to the watch room at ground level. He ignored the enormous circular space and its new modular furnishings as he fixed his attention on the highly polished wooden wall, where the force ran strongest. The bark itself had sight, a transparency by which he could see through the layers of wood to the world beyond, at will. He looked out, as he had done so many thousands of times in the past.

Outside, two females engaged in conversation. He immediately recognized Claire Grant. The old lady had been bragging everywhere she went about how her granddaughter, Emma, had designed a sculpture for Tyler's historic town square and oldest park.

Venn's park, not the town's.

But he'd lost that battle a long time ago, and until recently, he had managed to direct the city officials' attentions elsewhere. Damn their renewed interest. The tree had been marked for preservation purposes, which was a good thing, yet it also attracted unwanted attention. There were others who had an inclination of the riches the tree held, not in monetary value but in what they could do with the knowledge contained within.

The presumed granddaughter turned.

Venn advanced to the barrier, curious. He wanted to be closer to her, wanted nothing between them, not this tree, not this space. With his extraordinary sight and hearing, he could make her out perfectly, but it wasn't enough. There was something about her...yet he couldn't fathom why he'd be drawn Claire Grant's granddaughter. How odd.

With a sweeping glance, the young woman arched her brows and strolled toward the tree. She seemed to stare right at him. Thick auburn hair draped over her shoulders, and she tilted her head, his equilibrium shattering. A roar took up residence inside his skull. Thunder vibrated through his chest, and explosive desire made him hard and ready.

His breath hitched. His inner beasts stirred without the customary summons, fighting each other, wolf and hawk vying for a glimpse of her.

She inched forward.

Yes, move closer.

She spoke, and he vaguely caught her whispered French phrase. *"Coeur de mon coeur."*

Heart of my heart.

He swallowed, hard.

She placed a delicate palm on the trunk, and Venn growled as a surge of energy—her very essence—flowed into the tree, filled him as much as earthy air filled his lungs.

"I...feel something," Emma said with opened-mouth awe. "The oak has been here for hundreds of years."

When recognition hit Venn, it was with the force of an 18-wheeler rear-ending a car waiting at a traffic light. Every muscle in his body tensed as he saw flashes of her in a past life, of their limbs entwined, of her lips warm on his, of her vibrant laugh...of her dying.

Could it truly be Amelia? Had she returned to him in this woman, this Emma Grant?

Venn closed his eyes and summoned energy in all its manifested forms—heat, light, sound, magnetism, gravity, and all of life's functions—reaching out to her, touching deep into her soul to test the theory. Her initial response was a lazy yawn, but then her mystical imprint danced, the spirit unique to her, proclaimed, *Yes!*

She. Was. His.

A heaviness slammed against his chest, followed by whiplash, pain, confusion. He'd been robbed of time, his woman, his love.

Ah, Amelia. Brought back to him after so long.

A spark flared in his chest, and his pulse sped up. Unwilling to move lest this sudden feel-good moment disappeared, he held his breath.

She glanced over her shoulder at her grandmother. "I have the strangest feeling of déjà vu."

Overwhelmed, he wished he could vault through the barrier and take her in his arms. Instead, he braced both hands on thick chair arms as he slowly lowered himself into the seat, not taking his eyes off the woman with fiery hair and golden skin. Every fiber in his body stretched out to embrace her. She was his.

They'd been lovers in 1809. Companions. Promised journey mates. A favor from God.

His throat tightened at the memory, and he tried to drink in the air. She was the one woman gifted with the powers to complement his. He hadn't known until too late how much he needed to share his life with someone. And his enemy had murdered her.

She must be the reason the tree summoned him.

He narrowed his eyes, scrutinizing the grounds for yet another assassin. But the only ones there were the Grants.

Uncertain what to expect, he watched, fisting his hand with a vow.

This time he would protect her. This time he would fulfill the promise of a lifetime mate. This time she would be his. Forever.

Emma's brow furrowed as her hand swept along the bark of the tree. *His* tree. "Did I come here as a girl?" she asked. "I seem to know this place."

"I don't think so, child. Your father didn't wander much south of the ravine. Claimed he got bad vibes here. Always afraid, that boy. Not enough faith. Of course, there were all kinds of stories bantered about back then. Some about a man being killed out here, tales about witches and ghosts, you name it. The place became run-down. But with the city rejuvenation and cleanup, well… As you can see, things are different now."

Indeed, things had changed, Venn mused. His mansion lay south of the park, far enough away so as to not attract visitors. A strategic plan he'd sanctioned to assure his privacy. Back in the day, he'd met with wealthy plantation owners and connected politicians on his own terms. Otherwise, he'd avoided them. As time passed and with the never-ending urbanization, he didn't care for the coziness.

When Emma pulled her hand away from the bark, it was like part of him flickered, then snuffed out. He got a mild case of shakes, and his temperature plummeted.

"It's getting late, you must be tired," Mrs. Grant said.

"Nah. I'm a night person, remember? How about if we stop by Aunt Fay's Coffee Shop on the way home? I've been dreaming about one of her famous cinnamon buns all the way here."

"Okay. You drive." She hitched the small dog she held higher under her arm.

They were leaving. With a leap, Venn stood, banging his knee on the side table. He winced and beat back a wave of anxiety. He'd been given a second chance and he'd be damned if he'd let her out of his sight this time. At least, not for long.

Keenly aware that she wouldn't know him in this life, he needed to initiate a meeting. This minute. However, walking up out of nowhere in a shabby park might scare her.

He wished they could simply pick up where they'd left off.

He envisioned her smiling at him with recognition and running into his opened arms.

But as she got closer to the car and farther from him, the vision scattered.

Aunt Fay's. That was it.

He could use a jolt of caffeine.

AWAKENING FIRE is available now!

ACKNOWLEDGMENTS

Many thanks to my fabulous team of professionals:

Cover design: Dreams2media
Interior formatting: Author E.M.S.
Editor: Danielle Poiesz
Editor and proofreader: Cynthia Shepp

About the Author

Larissa Emerald has always had a powerful creative streak whether it's altering sewing patterns, or the need to make some minor change in recipes, or frequently rearranging her home furnishings, she relishes those little walks on the wild side to offset her otherwise quite ordinary life. Her eclectic taste in books cover numerous genres, and she writes sexy contemporary romance, paranormal romance, and futuristic romantic thrillers. But no matter the genre or time period, she likes strong women in dire situations who find the one man who will adore her beyond reason and give up everything for true love.

Larissa is happy to connect with her readers. Stop by and say hello at her website, Facebook, Twitter, or send her an email: larissaemerald@gmail.com.